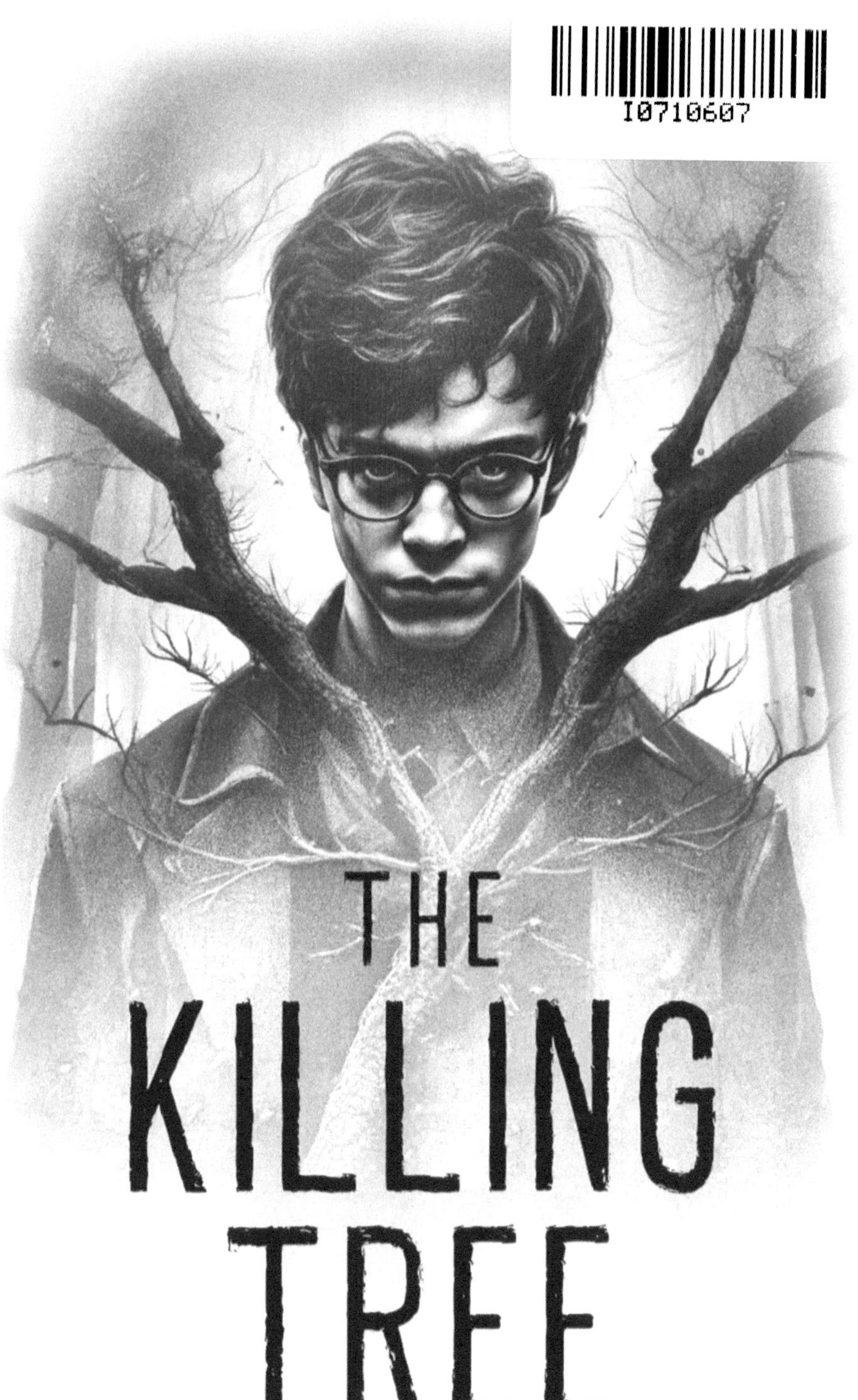
I0710607
THE
KILLING
TREE

HOLLY KNIGHTLEY

THE KILLING TREE

For my brother, Johnny

CONTENTS

CHAPTER ONE: *The Confession* 1

CHAPTER TWO: *My Tree* 7

CHAPTER THREE: *The Winter Festival* 21

CHAPTER FOUR: *White Orbs* 31

CHAPTER FIVE: *Mr. Brentley's House* 44

CHAPTER SIX: *Evelyn Butler's House* 54

CHAPTER SEVEN: *Cookies and Milk* 62

CHAPTER EIGHT: *A Warning* 69

CHAPTER NINE: *A Wish* 82

CHAPTER TEN: *The Day after Christmas* 85

CHAPTER ELEVEN: *The Truth* 87

CHAPTER ONE
The Confession

Hitch came into our dorm room frantic. He did that from time to time and I didn't pay much attention. He was a film major, to which he said he had no choice in the matter. The stars foretold his greatness, owing to the fact he was born under the last name Hitchcock. He always said his mother did him a great injustice not naming him after the famous film director Alfred Hitchcock. He commented ad nauseam how great it would be to be called Alfred Hitchcock II versus Charles Alphonse Hitchcock. He settled for Charlie Hitch and was known simply as Hitch to his closest friends.

Hitch rushed to his oversize safe at the foot of his bed. He turned the combination as if he was defusing a bomb. It housed his blue binder that contained all of his movie ideas, scripts, trade secrets, and probably a key to another dimension. Before the mammoth safe, the binder was tucked under his bed. That was until his paranoia got the best of him and he sprang for the safe. On more than a few occasions some of his film buddies would attempt to break into it or move it to mess with him, but to no avail. Hitch's blue binder would survive an atomic bomb.

After thumbing through his binder in genuine concentration, with beads of sweat dripping from his furrowed brow, he threw it on the floor. With a dramatic freefall that produced a groan that made it sound like we may have seen the last of his bed, he outstretched his arms to an invisible god. "Why?! Why have you forsaken me!"

"Everything okay Hitch?" I asked from my desk where I was busy working on Chemistry IV equations for my final exam that Friday.

"No! Life as I know it is over. *The Stranger*'s been slashed."

"Slashed as in shelved?" I asked, trying to keep up.

The Stranger was his senior film project he'd been working on since the beginning of the semester. He spent every waking moment either working on it or talking about it. It had dawned on me long ago, I could've gotten a minor in film just from his secondhand knowledge. That might have looked really good on my medical school applications, but it didn't matter, I'd already attained early acceptance to Stanford Medical for next fall.

"Yes, shelved. The old girl has been put where all films go to die."

"It can't be that bad," I assured him, not looking up from my study guide. "You loved it last week. I'm sure whatever it is you don't like now can be fixed in edits."

I felt his eyes boring holes into my back. I turned around to face him. His eyes looked like storm clouds; they were calling for rain. Maybe it *was* that bad.

"It's bad. Jill's the worst actress in the history of the world! Directing is good, the story is good, but the acting . . . the acting is shit!"

I held back my comment about the director directing the actors. "Can't you just reshoot Jill's scenes?"

"Oh Knox, you have all the answers, don't you?!" He placed his pillow over his face and screamed into it.

I knew cutting Jill from *The Stranger* was out of the

question. Jill was Hitch's girlfriend and if she didn't have that title, at the very least, she was his good friend with benefits. Though I was convinced one day Hitch would be big in the movie industry and have starlets on his arms everywhere he went, right now he was the closest thing to a real-life girl repellent I'd ever seen. For as fun as Hitch is, he's just as unattractive. Like his idol, he's husky with a nose that resembles a beak. To complete his look, he shaves his red hair, showing the world a shiny scalp that could serve as a makeshift mirror.

I didn't agree, but Hitch was convinced I could play a heartthrob if I ditched the glasses and what he dubbed 'the science stuff,' not that I wore a pocket protector or anything. It was true, I'd filled out since high school and was no longer short and scrawny, but a heartthrob I was not.

After what happened with Evelyn Butler in high school, I couldn't talk to girls without my mouth getting dry and my palms beading up with sweat. I was pretty sure everyone at school thought I had a glandular problem. I essentially assigned myself to die a virgin and had come to terms with that.

"It's not only Jill," Hitch said, removing the pillow from half of his face and fixating on me with his exposed eye. "The Stranger, the actual person, as in the killer, is awful! If there was someone in charge of casting, I'd fire them." He moaned into the pillow, "I don't get it. Gerald was so good at tryouts! As soon as the camera cuts to him, he freezes up."

Hitch tossed aside the pillow and propped himself up on his elbows. "You know what, you could play the killer. You'd be perfect! You already have all the creepy mannerisms down. You'd be like another Ted Bundy."

I turned away from Hitch and went back to studying. Two people couldn't be more different. I was very quiet, to the point of strange, but I wouldn't call my mannerisms creepy. Freshman year,

Hitch probably would've traded rooms with someone the first chance he got if it weren't for my name, or more precisely my last name which I share with the late actress Angela Lansbury. He took it as a sign. Just as the stars had laid out his favorable fate in Hollywood, they foretold our everlasting friendship. Roommates both having Hollywood royalty surnames had to mean something.

Hitch pulled himself from his bed and hovered by my desk. "What you say buddy ole' pal, will you do it?"

"I don't appreciate being compared to a serial killer."

"I wasn't comparing you, not really. And being the next Ted Bundy wouldn't be a bad thing. He did get all the ladies, if only to kill them. Besides, it's just a movie."

I didn't respond.

He put his hand to his forehead and pretended to faint. "It's not always about you Knox Lansbury. This is my life. You think as my best friend you'd help me out. Let's reshoot with you as the killer?"

I shook my head without looking up.

"Please."

"No," I said, not entertaining it.

He laced his fingers together as if in prayer. "Pretty please? I'll even let you wear your glasses."

He pulled my glasses off to examine them. "These may give off a glare in some scenes. We may have to visit the props department."

I snatched back my glasses, "I said no."

Again, he threw himself onto his bed. A horrible squeaking noise pursued as he rocked himself back and forth like he was strapped into a straitjacket. The noise made the muscles in my back tense. "Why not? Give me one good reason. We both know you don't have to study."

Heat rushed to my face and cheeks, ultimately reaching the

tips of my ears. I had held my secret so close for so long, I suppose sooner or later it had to come out. Secrets like mine always do. Ted Bundy's did.

"What is it?" Hitch asked, no doubt noticing the color change in my complexion. I was unvaryingly even mannered; not letting things get to me. I preferred it that way, to fly under the radar and blend into my surroundings like a chameleon. Maybe I *would* be a good actor . . . or good serial killer for that matter.

I trusted Hitch more than anyone in the world. He had long ago become my best friend. And there was this part of me that wanted to tell someone, and a smaller part that wanted to tell everyone. "Hitch I can't play a killer because . . ."

"Because?"

It was now, or never. If I wanted to get it off my chest, this was my chance. I shut my textbook and looked Hitch dead in the eyes, his blue eyes twinkling with hope. "I can't play a killer because *I am* a killer . . . It's all just to real for me."

I let my back conform to my seat as my shoulders sagged forward. It was finally out. My dark secret had come to see the light of day.

I deserved every reprehensible thought Hitch could think upon hearing such a confession. It couldn't be worse than my own nocturnal condemnations. Murder is wrong. It's the most loathsome of human behavior. In fact, it's not human at all—it's animalistic. We, as a species, have evolved above this basic 'fight to live' principle that Charles Darwin outlined in *The Origin of Species.* Being human defies the scientific principle of survival of the fittest.

Hitch snorted a high pitch laugh. It wasn't his normal laugh; it was sprinkled with anxiety as if part of him believed I *could* be a killer.

"You're pulling my leg," he said, a smile tugging at the corners of his lips until he was grinning like the Cheshire Cat. He always did that, smiled ear to ear when he was particularly proud of something he said and always when he used a line he would consider to be 'in the business.' "I see what's happening here, Gerald knew he was on the chopping block and asked you to say no. Knox, you're a better actor than I thought. You *have to* play the part now!"

I shook my head, trying to make my point. "Gerald didn't put me up to it. I murdered my brother."

His shoulders slumped, his double chin now resting on his chest. "You told me a tree fell on him."

"Both are true."

He disingenuously acted intrigued, sitting tall in his bed. "Let me guess, you pushed it on him. Wait, no, you lured him there divining it was going to fall. Or the most likely, you drugged him, then placed him under the tree, then timber!"

"It didn't happen like that."

"How *did* it happen?" he asked incredulously.

Returning to my study guide, "Forget it."

My entire face felt like it was on fire. My heart pounded in my chest as it reverberated in my ears. I regretted opening my mouth. Telling Hitch my secret didn't make me feel any better, if anything I felt worse. Admitting to Lincoln's murder out loud made me feel like a killer. I was, I knew that. How could I ever forget, but to feel it take a hold of me again made me lightheaded.

"Knox tell me," Hitch nagged, his voice taking on a high-pitched tone. "You can't say something like that and not elaborate."

"I can't tell you the truth, you'd never believe me."

He let out a noise that rivaled a rhinoceros at the zoo.

"I can't tell you, but I can show you."

CHAPTER TWO
My Tree

"You really have grown up so handsome," my mother cooed as she kissed the side of my face for what seemed like the hundredth time. I hadn't seen her in nearly four years, and she was making sure I received all of her belated hugs and kisses. After Lincoln's death, I chose to go to college in California. I wanted to get as far away from my family home as possible. If studying abroad was an option, I would have opted for that.

My mother's fear of flying played in perfectly with my need to self-ostracize myself from my family. Driving to California from New Jersey was practically impossible for my mother to do on her own and my father couldn't leave the tree farm long enough to drive cross country. I kept my parents at bay with a once-a-week video call to my mother and avoided any visits they would've deemed necessary if they didn't hear from me on a regular basis. This ensured my college years lulled on in a false sense of peace.

Before I walked out the front door, my mother pulled my scarf, forcing me to bend down to receive another embarrassing kiss. Hitch grinned as she balanced her affection, planting yet another kiss on the other side of my face and smashing my glasses against my cheekbone.

Hitch pinched the cheek, I wasn't rubbing. "Your boy's a real cutie. I always say so."

My father, who was reading the newspaper at the kitchen table, glanced our way.

I shrugged it off, "It's not like that, Dad."

"Sure it is," Hitch said, teasingly imitating my mother and acting as if he was going to kiss my cheek.

I pushed him out the front door before his lips touched skin. "What the heck was that about?! It's been four years since I've been home—are you trying to get me thrown out?!"

Hitch unzipped his black backpack and pulled out his camcorder. "It was a joke. Your mom thought it was funny. Your dad just needs to lighten up."

"He can't," I said, tucking my scarf into my winter coat.

I took the porch steps in a hurry, setting the rocking chairs in motion as I flew by. Hitch followed me, almost falling down the three steps that were a little icy. He was on my heels as I made my way behind the house in the direction of my family's tree farm. A heavy frost covered the grass, it crunched under my feet like broken glass. I quickened my pace, making a sharp right and took the dirt road that divided the family farm in half.

Frost had kissed the tops of the pines. The morning sun made it appear as if the trees were dipped in glitter. I had to smile. I missed this.

In the week building up to winter break, I'd dreamed of home. With the crispest clarity, I saw the perfect rows of trees. I smelled the familiar scent of Fir trees, recalling how the smell got into my hair in clothes. I could almost smell the sweet sap that lingered in the open country air this time of year as we harvested Christmas trees and bound garland for the holidays.

Hitch jogged to catch up with me. "So, why can't your dad relax? What's he in the final stages of—I got a stick up my ass?"

Hitch asked, camcorder in hand, backpack slung over his shoulder.

"Because he knows I killed Lincoln or at least he thinks I had something to do with it. He changed after Lincoln died. I guess I'm to blame for that too."

The truth was I thought my father hated me, but I couldn't say that out loud, not to Hitch and certainly not to my mother. I only ever thought it when I was in one of my dark moods and the little lies I told myself to keep me happy started to unravel.

Hitch turned on the camcorder, the little green light flashing. "Can you repeat that?"

"You're not seriously going to record me?"

"That was our deal. I'm skipping out on Christmas with my family for this. You don't understand how upset my dad is."

"I thought you're Jewish?"

"My mom is, but my dad plays the Santa every year in the town parade. I'm his half Jewish elf."

Hitch would be a great elf thanks to his squat figure. I could see him handing out dreidels to disappointed children who asked Santa for Xboxes.

"My mother understood this film is a matter of life or death, but this year Keyport is going to have a sad Santa without his little helper."

"I don't know what you're hoping to get from filming me. Maybe you should just fly home."

"I'm hoping to get raw emotion. Documentaries of guilt are big right now. I want to delve into the mental health crisis affecting America's youth."

I narrowed my eyes. "Hitch, you should fly home."

Disregarding me, "I want you to be candid, well after you say the first line that is. You remember your line, right?"

A cloud of hot breath escaped my lips like a smoking chimney. "I remember the line."

"Good," he said, focusing the camera on the neat rows of trees. "I just want to let you know I googled your brother after your little confession. Call it a safety precaution."

I raised an eyebrow. I didn't think he actually believed me.

"There was nothing suspicious about your brother's death. It was a freak accident, so I hope you have the guilty conscience angle planned out. If not, I suggest you stick to survivor's guilt."

"Isn't there a famous line about not trusting what you hear?" I asked, the quote on the tip of my tongue.

"That would be Edgar Allan Poe. He was one of Alfred Hitchcock's biggest influences." Hitch went on to quote the writer: "*Believe nothing you hear, and only one half that you see.*"

I ran my gloved hand across a Douglas Fir as I passed, "Well then, wait until you see."

"I don't care what I see, I care what the camera sees."

"Isn't that the same thing?"

"No. The camera always sees things differently. People and places conform to its magic."

I shook my head.

"I'll give it to you Knox, it's really pretty here. The camera is loving all of the Christmas trees. I always wanted to make a Christmas movie. Something you could watch every year like *Die Hard.*"

"You're going to be disappointed. The camera's not going to transform me into Bruce Willis."

Hitch laughed. "Wait till edits!"

"It's funny," I said, looking down at my feet, avoiding the trees for the moment. "I always thought the farm was sad."

"Only you could think a Christmas tree farm is sad Knox."

"Think about it; all the trees are waiting to be executed. They know they're condemned. They see their neighbors being cut down or dug up and all they can do is wait their turn."

"That's pretty morbid. Maybe you *are* a killer."

"The whole thing *is* morbid. They're cut down and placed inside homes where they get about a month of admiration before they're thrown out with the trash. But I guess it's better to be loved than never to be loved at all."

"That's not quite how Alfred, Lord Tennyson said it.

I envy not in any moods
The captive void of noble rage,
The linnet born within the cage,
That never knew the summer woods:
I envy not the beast that takes
His licence in the field of time,
Unfetter'd by the sense of crime,
To whom a conscience never wakes;
Nor, what may count itself as blest,
The heart that never plighted troth
But stagnates in the weeds of sloth;
Nor any want-begotten rest.
I hold it true, whate'er befall;
I feel it, when I sorrow most:
'Tis better to have loved and lost
Than never to have loved at all."

Hitch never ceased to amaze me. He'd do things like that from time to time, recite poetry or quote monologues from movies or books. Hitch was right about this one, I misquoted the famous line. But my misquote raised a question. Was it better to be loved or to be the one who loved? Was it better to be Lincoln, who everyone loved and admired like a Christmas tree to only be cut down before his time, or was it better to be me who'd loved him so much and now had to live on without him?

We walked on in silence until the dirt road ended, marking the end of Lansbury Tree Farm.

"This is Mr. Brentley's property," I said, pointing at the no trespassing signs attached to a barbed wired fence. There was a sign posted every few feet down the property line.

"Geez, somebody doesn't want to be disturbed. I think one sign would've gotten the point across."

"Mr. Brentley is the definition of a recluse. He's the wealthiest man in Elwood. In fact, he owns most of it. He used to operate a tree farm on his own land, but I guess it got to be too much for him. He sold off a chunk of his farm to my parents and they kept the tree farm alive."

We turned right, traveling along the fence. "We're almost there," I informed Hitch whose cheeks were already chapped from the wind. "What I want to show you borders Mr. Brentley's property and Lansbury Tree Farm."

"Good, I don't know how much more walking I can take. Jersey is nothing like the movies."

"You're thinking of North Jersey. South Jersey might as well be a different planet."

He adjusted his backpack, which had slid down his shoulder. "Makes sense. I never understood how the location of The *Sopranos* was filmed in the Garden State."

"There were some woodsy episodes, South Jersey acted as the *Sopranos* body dumpster."

Hitch nodded. "Yeah, I'm sensing that. You could bury a lot of bodies out here."

I abruptly stopped. Hitch bumped into me as he viewed the landscape through the camera lens, pushing me forward. I planted my feet and pointed up, "We're here." My voice sounded funny to my ears as if I was hearing it underwater. I wondered if Hitch noticed or if it was in my head.

I couldn't ask, I could only stare. Among the boundless Fir trees on Mr. Brentley's side of the fence stood a huge, dead tree that decades ago had grown through the fence. The chained links and barbed wire were now part of its trunk and jutted from it like body piercings.

"Wow," Hitch said, looking up at it in amazement, "that's one huge tree."

I nodded; my eyes still fixed upward. This particular tree had always captivated me. On our entire property and Mr. Brentley's, as far as I could see were Fir trees. We had Douglas Fir, Fraser Fir, Balsam Fir, Grand Fir, and White Fir trees. This tree was not in the Fir family, or even an evergreen. I wasn't entirely sure what type of tree it had been, but I knew it never would've cut it as a Christmas tree. The tree had a massively thick trunk turned ashen in age. Its fleshy branches gave off tiny fingerlike projections. The way the branches interconnected had always reminded me of a spider's web waiting for some unsuspecting insect to fly its way.

In a whisper, talking more to myself than Hitch, "This was my favorite spot when I was a boy. This was my tree. I would sit in front of this odd tree and feel like I had something in common with it. In a field of beautiful Christmas trees, we were the only ones different."

"That's not a bad thing. The field goes to the executioner after all," he said, reinventing my verbage from earlier.

"Just like my brother."

"About that," Hitch said, still fixated on the tree, "I thought the tree fell on him . . . I guess it was only a branch?"

I shook my head, he had it all wrong.

Hitch instinctively took a step back as if he was afraid he'd share the same fate as my brother. The camera lens focused on me. He mouthed: "Give me the first line."

My tongue was already sticking to the roof of my mouth. I

was no better than Gerald.

"Give me the first line," he repeated in a whisper.

I recited my one and only line. "This is the story of how I murdered my brother."

Hitch nodded. He indicated for me to go on, with the spinning of his finger in a circle. It reminded me of the hand gesture my brother and I would use to signal someone was crazy.

I cleared my throat. "I wished for the tree to kill my brother."

Hitch smiled and mouthed: "Did it?"

"Yes. The next day my brother died."

"Start in the beginning," he said in a whisper.

I wasn't sure why he was whispering. If he was going to edit himself out, what did it matter how loud he was and if he wasn't going to edit himself out, didn't he want to be heard? I knew Hitch knew what he was doing, so I'd trust the process.

"Why did you ask the tree to kill your brother?" Hitch asked, prompting me to continue.

"Because of Evelyn Butler." I restated the question and answer for the camera. "I asked for the tree to kill my brother because of Evelyn Butler."

Hitch gave me a thumbs up and mouthed: "Loving the sex appeal add in."

His finger was spinning again. He wanted me to elaborate. "Evelyn was the first girl I loved." I paused to think of Evelyn Butler. She was the only one. My childish heart beat for her since grade school. "I asked her to prom, and she said yes . . ."

I hadn't anticipated talking about Evelyn. Being home and saying her name made my hands beyond sweaty; they were scorching. I pulled off my gloves as if they were made of fire, throwing them to the ground. The cool air was refreshing, giving me the jolt I needed to continue. "I, uh . . . um, it took me weeks to get up the courage. During football season I'd talked to her a few times, giving me just enough push to ask her. Evelyn, like everyone in school, went to see Lincoln play, but we kept finding ourselves seated next to each other."

"Who's Lincoln?" Hitch whispered. "Introduce him."

"Lincoln's my brother, the one, the one I murdered," I stammered, as if there were more brothers waiting their turn.

Hitch's finger made a revolving circle again.

"Lincoln was my younger brother. We were Irish twins. He was less than a year younger than me. We were best friends despite our different friend circles. Me having none and him being popular as you'd imagine any high school quarterback would be. But Lincoln never left me behind. He was the very best and I, I loved him."

I took off my glasses and cleaned them with the bit of my scarf that hung from my coat. "We looked nothing alike. Maybe a little now. We both resemble my mother, but I have my father's dark hair. Well, Lincoln did resemble her," I said, sliding my glasses back on and gazing into the camera. I froze, entranced by the green, rhythmic blink of the camcorder.

"Evelyn," Hitch whispered.

"Yes, Evelyn. She said she'd go with me to prom. Lincoln had just broken up with his girlfriend and decided to tag along with Evelyn and me, despite the fact he could have gone with anyone. Anyone would've broken it off with their date to go with him."

"Speed it up," Hitch whispered. His finger circling double time.

"Uh, so at prom Evelyn went to the bathroom and was gone for a long time. I went to look for her and was about to give up when I heard her laugh. I'd know that laugh anywhere. It's this high pitch, cute laugh that sounds . . . I don't know, like a bubble popping. So, I, uh, followed her laugh down a hall and there she was in Lincoln's arms. I watched them kiss, that was until Lincoln noticed me."

I glanced over the trees of my family's farm remembering what I had tried to forget. I took a deep breath, the cold air stinging my lungs. "At first, I was shocked, then I was furious. Lincoln knew what she meant to me. He could have had anyone, why did he have to take her?"

Hitch nodded, calling for more. I ignored him. I was lost in the past. I could see Lincoln's face when he was discovered, how it twisted up in pain, how he pushed Evelyn off of him like she was a disease.

I looked at the camera dead on, "I remember feeling numb as I caught a car ride home. A group of kids were leaving prom early to party and were kind enough to drop me off on my street. I didn't want my parents to know I'd left early. I didn't want to face them. Instead, I ran down the road that divided our tree farm. The one we just walked down and ran along Mr. Brentley's property until I got to my tree. I basically threw my arms around the dead tree as if it could comfort me."

I touched my cheek, recalling the feel of the rough bark against my tearstained face. I glanced behind me and shuttered, the past ripping through me like a whirlwind. "That's when I said it."

"Said what?" Hitch asked, forgetting to whisper.

"I said it over and over again: I wish my brother was dead."

I looked past the camera at Hitch. All I could see was his shoulders, the lower half of his face hidden behind his plaid scarf.

"I know what you're thinking, but you're wrong. It wasn't a coincidence. The next day, I was with my father and Lincoln, we were pruning the trees which we always did on the weekends, when Lincoln broke formation to talk to me after the silent treatment I'd given him at breakfast. I didn't want to have that conversation in front of my parents. Usually, we each took a row of trees and moved our way down the rows together. But there Lincoln was, wanting to talk. I'll never forget what he said when I asked him why he did it. He said: *Because I could. Because she wanted me, and I could.*"

I ran my hand down my face in remembrance. "I turned away from him, giving him the cold shoulder; I couldn't stand to look at him. I couldn't believe he'd do that to his own brother. To his best friend."

"*I'm sorry,* he'd said to me in a soft voice I never heard him used before. *Can you forgive me?*"

I paused for a long time, forgetting about Hitch and his camera. How clearly I could still hear Lincoln's voice. *Can you forgive me?*

Hitch snapped his fingers. Stirred to my purpose, my head bobbed up, my eyes locking with the camera. I spoke as if on cue, as if I was just another one of his actors. "Before I could answer Lincoln, the tree in the row next to us fell over and crushed my brother. The sound of the trunk snapping, the fibers of the tree tearing apart seemed like an aftershock. I didn't perceive the noise until the tree had fallen. My father, he must've heard the tree snap or maybe it was my scream, for at that point, I realized I was screaming. Screaming at the top of my lungs. My message, a jumbled call for help and for my brother. My father yelled for me to assist him, his hands already yanking on the fallen tree. I came to my senses and together we rolled the tree off of Lincoln. We were too late. He was dead."

With the utmost vivid detail, I recalled my brother lying in the dirt, how the stray pine needles littered his light hair in slashes of green as a red cut bloomed across his handsome face. His blue eyes were wide open. They looked like glass under the frames of his dark lashes. Like broken glass. Little spider webs of red bled in from the corners of his eyes until it consumed them in blood. It was an image I tried not to conjure, but I couldn't help it. Lincoln—dead— was burnt into the back of my eyelids. Every time I closed my eyes, even the split second required to blink, Lincoln was with me. Running to California couldn't stop that. Lincoln's death was a part of who I am.

Again, I looked behind me at the tree, at my tree, my eyes running down the gray-colored bark as if it held some answer. "I never got the chance to tell Lincoln I forgave him."

I let out my breath slowly, watching it billow into the cold air. "Some expert came out and said the tree had ant damage and that's why it fell but that wasn't true. We spray for ants. The tree just fell." My hands tightened into fist at my sides. "But trees don't just fall. I'd know. Trees are my family's business. My brother and I grew up on this tree farm and we never had a tree *just* fall. My tree made it happen," I said, turning around to point an accusatory finger at it. "It granted my wish." I could feel the heat on my face as I focused my attention back on the camera. My entire body was slick with sweat, the tips of my ears burning as if they caught on fire.

"The next day I overheard my father talking to my mother. He told her Lincoln was dead because of me, because I made him break formation and if it weren't for me, he'd still be alive. I knew he was upset; we all were. It was one thing to think it was my fault and another to hear my father say it was. I darted out the front door and to the one place I always felt I belonged. But when I reached my tree . . ."

"Yes," Hitch said, zooming in.

"The branches that had always reminded me of spider webs had changed. Somehow the branches had twisted to form my brother's face."

"What did you do?" Hitch asked, so caught up he forgot to whisper.

"I ran. I ran and I never came back, that was until today."

"I don't see a face in the branches," Hitch said, focusing the camera up.

"I don't either," I acknowledged. "Just the spider webs catching their prey."

"Maybe it was just guilt making you see things."

"I think you're right. I think it was the guilt," I said, meaning it. I laughed at myself. "Of course it was the guilt. How can a tree grant a wish? All these years I avoided coming home to face my tree and my parents because I thought I was a murderer." I laughed again, my giggle of a laugh filling the quiet tree farm, and I realized the only sound on the farm was me—my goofy laugh. There were no birds chirping. Not a one. At Standford we had tons of birds and squirrels; had the farm always been so silent?

I cleared my throat, focusing on the camera. "I understand now. Everything I thought happened was just an elaborate concoction of my brain to punish myself. It wasn't enough to take the blame for Lincoln being at the wrong place at the wrong time, I had to add a ridiculous story on top of it. A story that pushed me away from my home and my family. It was all just self-inflicted punishment. The idea that a tree fulfilled some dark wish is crazy, and as a future doctor I'm ashamed of myself for believing it for so long. Thanks Hitch, for helping me come to my senses. I should've faced reality a long time ago. My brother, Lincoln David Lansbury, died at age seventeen when a tree fell and crushed him. It was a freak accident, and I had nothing to do with it."

"Do you feel better now that you got that off your chest?"

I shook my head, strands of my dark hair falling over my glasses. I brushed them back. "Not really. I faced my fears and can move on from that. I no longer have to avoid coming home, but the guilt, the guilt I will always carry with me."

"If your father wants to blame you, that's a him problem. You didn't force Lincoln to break formation that day, Lincoln did that. And as far as the creepy tree, you said a stupid thing and it happened. It's what we in the business call Kafkaesque. It was just a bizarre coincidence. You can't beat yourself up over it. Your brother knew you loved him."

I stared off into the horizon as if it could take me to the past. "I regret so much about that day. It seems so stupid to have put all of the blame on my brother. It was just as much Evelyn's fault as his. I could have spared myself so much guilt if I never said it. I wish I could go back in time. Instead of Lincoln, I'd wish for Evelyn Butler to die."

CHAPTER THREE

The Winter Festival

"Vinter Wonderland," Hitch read off the sign as we pulled into the local winery. "Is this a beer festival or a wine tasting thing?"

I slowed my mother's pumpkin spice Dodge Caliber to a crawl. Pedestrians were coming and going, cutting through the traffic to get to the winery or the parking lot respectively. "It's a German Christmas theme festival at a winery. You should be able to get wine or beer."

"There's no time like the holidays to get your drink on. Family togetherness can drive anyone to drink."

A faint smile curled up the corner of my mouth, I knew he was talking about my family in particular. Hitch seemed pleased he pulled a smile out of me, even if it was a feeble one. Since the morning, I'd been moody and quieter than my usual, which was basically silent.

I went for a crack of my own. "The pressure of having your dad as Santa must really make you thirsty."

He laughed. "I travel with an eggnog canteen."

Parking in the first available parking spot I found, we got out of the Dodge to a cold winter night. Stars already dappled the dark sky, and the pale moon rose high above the winery in an unmistakable grin.

I hurriedly put on my gloves as we walked. I wasn't used to Jersey winters anymore. I glanced at Hitch, I could tell he was having a hard time with the cold too. He had pulled his beanie over his ears and the bulk of his forehead.

"Wishing you didn't shave your hair right about now?"

"*Beauty is pain.*"

"I don't know that one," I admitted. "Who said it?"

"It's a French saying, but Hollywood perfected it. *I must suffer to be beautiful.*"

I laughed; I couldn't help myself. "It looks like you have a lot more suffering to do."

"Laugh it up Ted Bundy."

I bit back another laugh, "I deserve that."

We approached the winery to see fire pits ablaze and groups of people in winter garb huddling around them for warmth. The sound of children playing as they sped around the ice-skating rink pierced the night like the shrill hoot of the barn owl. White lights on strings were wrapped around poles, lighting the way to small shops selling holiday wears, art, and refreshments.

Suddenly, I became overwhelmed. The sound of voices and laughter became deafening. The small lights seemed magnified, like I came face to face with a flood light. I wanted to leave.

I closed my eyes to steady my nerves. I saw Lincoln—dead. He was lying on the ground amongst fallen pine needles. The cut on his cheek unraveled in a thin crimson ribbon. His eyelids closed for a fraction of a heartbeat before opening again. His blue eyes were clouded over in red and in death. "Can you forgive me?"

My eyelids flashed open. I always saw my brother when I closed my eyes, that was nothing new. But he had never moved. Had never spoken. The stress of the day was really getting to me. That, and I just realized I hadn't eaten all day. I had been so nervous about making my video confession I skipped breakfast. My guilt was always the hardest to bear when I was worn down, physically or mentally and I was both. I just needed to eat something, and I'd be okay.

"Earth to Knox," Hitch said, nudging me. "You alright? You zoned out."

I scanned the food options: cookies, rice crispy treats, or chocolate covered pretzels. That wasn't going to cut it. I needed real food. There was no way I could down a beer without getting something solid in my stomach and sweets didn't count. "I want to leave."

Hitch breathed out through his nose like a dragon, two steady streams of hot air filling the night. "We just got here, and you told your mom you'd catch up with her."

I wasn't looking at Hitch but past him. I knew seeing and hearing Lincoln was in my head, but I couldn't help myself from scanning the throng for him.

"Are you sick?" Hitch slid off a glove to place his hand to my clammy forehead. "You're sweating and it's freezing out. That can't be a good sign, but you're the future doctor here not me."

"I just want to go. I'm tired and hungry. We can come back tomorrow. The festival runs until Christmas."

"It's probably for the best. I don't feel like hearing it from your mom that I kept her baby out when he wasn't feeling good," he said in a whiny voice imitating a spoiled brat. He turned upon his heels like a soldier following orders and headed back in the direction of the car. I followed.

We walked along a path lined by mature pitch pines that separated the parking lot from the winery's grape vines.

"Tomorrow we should rent one of those firepits and invite some of your friends out," Hitch said, trading in marching for something between walking and skipping.

"You're my only friend Hitch."

"Come on," he said with a playful elbow. "That can't be true."

I nodded, looking at the ground.

"What about Evelyn Butler? She still live around here?"

 "I guess you missed the little detail about her breaking my heart," I grumbled. "And I have no idea if Evelyn stayed local."

"Did I hear my name?" A voice said, coming from a group of girls walking toward the winery. The question was followed by a giggle.

I froze. I should have kept walking, but my feet became glued to the ground. I knew that voice. I knew that laugh. It was the sound of airy bubbles popping.

A girl broke away from the group and came my way. Confirmation—it was Evelyn Butler. She was unmistakable even in poor lighting. I internally prayed she didn't hear what I said about her breaking my heart. Evelyn had grown more beautiful, if that was even possible. In my mind, I had already made Evelyn Butler one of Homer's sirens—so beautiful you would let her lull you to death and be thankful for it.

Her crow dark hair fell in tight ringlets around her soft face. It was the perfect complement to her snow-white skin. Evelyn Butler would make the ideal Snow White. I'm sure Hitch would agree that her full face, bright red lips, and crisp blue eyes were made for the silver screen.

"Knox Lansbury," she said, recognizing me and throwing her arms around my neck. "I can't believe it's you! I ask your mom about you all the time."

"You . . . you do?" I stammered.

"Yes," she acknowledged, pulling herself away to get a better look at me. I felt disheveled under her gaze. I knew my scarf didn't match my gloves and my winter coat was one of my father's as I had no need for a heavy coat in California.

"My mother never told me," I said so after the point I wasn't sure if she understood what and why I said what I said.

I did wonder why that was. My mom kept me posted on everything else: Mrs. Ford's knee surgery, the Hickman twins marrying sisters, the church getting a new roof, etcetera, etcetera, etcetera.

Hitch took Evelyn's gloved hand and kissed it. "I'm Knox's *only* and *best* friend Charlie Hitch." She giggled, evidently pleased by his attention.

"Sorry, this is Hitch," I said, already recovered from the shock of seeing Evelyn Butler. "He's a little eccentric, he makes movies."

Evelyn's name was called by the group she came with. They stood on the other side of the car-wide path waiting for her.

"You know what Evelyn," Hitch said, still holding onto her hand. "I'm making a short film while I'm here visiting Knox for the holidays, and I have a part I think you'd be perfect for."

"Come on Evey!" Her friends called.

"Go ahead, I'll catch up with you guys later!" she yelled back.

I knew Hitch would agree Evelyn was pretty enough to be in a movie, but I didn't want her in his, in mine. I was beyond furious, heading toward enraged. Hitch didn't care. He ignored my elbow jabs and continued to shower Evelyn with compliments.

What sounded like a clap of thunder boomed overhead. It was so loud it resonated through me, physically shaking my body. I was scarcely aware of the tree branch falling before I lunged at Evelyn, tackling her to the ground. The tree branch crashed next to us, landing in splintered pieces, each piece large enough to have killed Evelyn.

Hitch helped her to her feet. "Are you okay?!"

She stood on shaking knees as I pulled myself from the ground. A crowd had formed around us. The many voices were drowned out to an incessant humming. A man dressed in black tugged on my arm. I noticed 'security' spelled out in white capital letters across his chest. "Do you need an ambulance?"

"No." My voice sounded like a yell ping ponging through my skull, though I was sure I spoke softly.

He asked Hitch and Evelyn the same question.

"I'm okay," she said. With a gesture in my direction, "He saved me."

I was too disoriented to appreciate her praise. I think she noticed.

"Knox, are you sure you're alright? You're bleeding?"

"Hmm?"

She ran her glove over the blood dripping down the side of my face and showed me. Her pink glove now had a streak of red on the index finger.

I instinctively put my hand to the cut to assess the extent of my injury. "It's just a scratch."

My adrenaline was still pumping. I didn't feel the cut, but I did feel her glove on my face and was sorry when she took it away.

The security guard, in a clipped tone, spoke into his walkie talkie asking for help with crowd control. "Move back," he hollered to the crowd who continued to gather. Show's over, go enjoy the festival!" Sharply, he turned to us. "If you don't want an ambulance called, can you three also move on. I need to get a crew in here to clear the branches."

"Not a problem," Hitch said cocky, presumably not liking the security guard's tone, "we were just leaving." His reaction may have subliminally had something to do with Alfred Hitchcock's fear of law enforcement. Every time a cop car whizzed by, Hitch always made it a point to tell me.

"Wait," the security guard said as his flashlight illuminated my face. "You're bleeding. I'm calling an ambulance."

"It's just a scratch," I repeated, before walking toward my mothers' vehicle.

"Wait, you have to fill out an accident report!" he yelled after me. "It's protocol. If a guest gets hurt on the property an accident report has to be filled out!"

I was glad for the crowd. I didn't think the security guard would chase after me, not even in the name of protocol. I waved my hand dismissively, "Nothing happened."

But did it? Did I make the tree branch fall and almost kill Evelyn Butler? I thought back to the morning, to the last thing I said into the camera: *I wish for Evelyn Butler to die.* No—that's absurd. I'd just gone through this with Lincoln. My tree can't grant wishes, it was just a coincidence. What did Hitch call it—Kafkaesque.

I was just about to mention the strange coincidence to Hitch when I realized it wasn't him walking next to me but Evelyn Butler. This confused me more than anything. Weren't her friends part of the crowd? Why was she walking with me and where was Hitch?

I glanced behind me to see Hitch with his camcorder in hand, filming the crowd.

"He said it's for the film he's working on."

"Oh," I said, still wondering why she was with me.

Evelyn, perhaps understanding my inflection, went on to explain her presence. "He asked me to walk you back to your car."

"Oh, uh, thank you, but I don't need an escort."

"I think you hit your head harder than you think. Maybe we should've let that guy call an ambulance."

"No," I said louder than I meant to.

When Lincoln died. There was an ambulance. The siren, with its flashing lights, whipped around the tree farm painting everything red. I couldn't live through that again.

I leaned against the Dodge waiting for Hitch. "I probably have a concussion, and there's nothing they can do for that anyway."

"Fine," she said, "no ambulance, but I'm going to at least clean the cut. I have a lot of practice with that over the years thanks to my mom."

That's right, Evelyn's mother had a drinking and drug problem that had landed her in more than a few scrapes over the years. I recalled that the few times I'd seen her as a child, she always had at least one visible Band-Aid.

"My mom's better now," Evelyn said, leaning next to me. "After what happen to Lincoln, she made it a point to get clean and has been ever since. Don't get me wrong, she's had a few slip ups here and there, but's she's well. Better than she's been in a long time."

I looked at her dazed. "Why would my brother's death mean anything to your mother?"

Evelyn's eyes went to the stars above us. "I had a hard time after what happened. My mom said she had to get clean to take care of me since I had taken care of her for so long."

It never crossed my mind that Evelyn would've struggled with Lincoln's death.

"Got what I needed," Hitch yelled, jogging back to the car. "Let's go check out the footage."

* * *

I sat on the couch in the living room as Hitch sat in front of the television, readying his camcorder to hook into the TV. It was proving more of a challenge than he first thought. My parents still had the same television as when I was a kid, and it lacked modern hookups. Hitch was sure, with a little movie ingenuity and elbow grease, he could get his camcorder to play on it.

"Found it," Evelyn announced, coming back into the living room with a bottle of peroxide and a box of Band-Aids.

Before sitting on the couch, she stopped at the Christmas tree in the corner. It was one of our own, cut down in preparation for my visit and decorated with all the ornaments children make their parents. She fixated on the ornament that was a frame made out of colored popsicle sticks. It housed a picture of Lincoln and me when I was about six, with our names written around the border: Knox Brent Lansbury and Lincoln David Lansbury.

Evelyn glanced at me where I sat in the middle of the couch and then back at the ornament, before taking a seat next to me, not that I gave her much of a choice with my middle position.

She took a tissue from the Kleenex box on the coffee table and poured peroxide onto it before dabbing the cut on the side of my temple.

"It burns."

"It's supposed to silly; it's killing the germs."

I smiled to myself. Duh. I didn't sound like a future doctor; I sounded like an idiot.

She reached for the box of Band-Aids. "Good news is, you're right about the cut not being deep, but I also think you're right about having a concussion."

"Maybe," I said, rubbing the side of my head. I had a vague impression of my head striking the ground when I nosedived for Evelyn, but maybe it was an accidental clash of heads.

"It's lucky you didn't break your glasses."

I took my glasses off to examine them. She was right, there wasn't a scratch on them. I went to put them back on, her soft touch stopping me. "You look so much like Lincoln without your glasses on. I never noticed it before. It's a little scary."

Evelyn brushed my dark hair away from my face. Her delicate fingertips sent little jolts through my skull. My body tensed in a good way. She peeled the back of the Band-Aid and placed it over my cut.

With her face close to mine, she whispered, keeping Hitch out of the conversation. "I didn't get a chance to apologize."

I didn't respond. I felt like I'd stopped breathing. Her lips were so close to my face, all I had to do was turn a little and our lips would touch.

"Knox, I'm sorry about Lincoln."

I remained facing forward, my eyes on Hitch as I spoke. "Are you sorry for kissing him or because he died the next day?"

"Both," she replied, her hot breath tingling the little hairs on my ear. I couldn't stand it, I scooted away from her, creating distance between us.

She scooted closer, keeping her voice in a whisper. "I always liked your brother. I hated football but never missed a game because of him. I went to the prom with you to be near him."

My eyes darted to her, angst, and regret, and guilt, and I don't know what else boiled inside of me. I didn't need to hear this. She used me to get to Lincoln. She never liked me. Knowing I wished for my brother to die over a girl who'd used me made me feel that much worse. A pain shot across my temple, as my guilt bubbled over, fixating in my heart. I hated Evelyn Butler.

She reached for my hand, I avoided her touch and donned my glasses. "Knox, I'm sorry I hurt you and caused bad blood between you and your brother. Can you ever for—"

"Knox, you're going to want to see this!" Hitch said, his voice reaching an unnaturally high note, bordering on shrill.

We looked toward the television.

CHAPTER FOUR

White Orbs

"What are we looking at?" Evelyn asked, moving to sit next to Hitch in front of the TV.

"It's footage from Lansbury Tree Farm from this morning."

She pointed at the small, white opaque bubbles dancing all over the screen. "What are those?"

I'd seen enough rough footage to know it was glare. "Glare," I said to her from the couch, waiting for Hitch to parrot me. But he didn't.

"No, that's not glare. They're perfect little orbs. Look how they weave in and out of the trees. There's no way that's from the sun reflecting off the frost. I can't believe I'm going to say this, but I think it's—"

"What?" Evelyn asked, so entranced she didn't seem to realize she'd cut Hitch off.

"I only saw it once and it was from cut footage from Hitchcock's Psycho. Only a select group of film students ever saw it before it went MIA." He looked off to the distance as if to pay respect to the lost footage. "I feel honored to have been among them."

"We all want to know Hitch, what is it?" I asked,

sarcastically. I'd heard it all being roommates with him for nearly four years. This was not the first time he claimed to have had access to some special, never to be seen again footage.

"I won't keep you waiting then," he said, locking eyes with me. "They're spirit orbs."

"Spirit orbs . . ." Evelyn repeated, enthralled.

"Yep, they say what you're actually looking at is a human soul or a ghost, your pick. They've been said to show up on the camera as bright, shining bubbles. Granted, I've only ever seen one once before, but it reminded me of a dying star floating haphazardly."

I joined Hitch and Evelyn in front of the TV, taking my place next to Hitch. I wasn't interested until he said ghost, my mind traveling to my brother. I chalked up what I saw at the winery when I closed my eyes to stress, stress from being back home and making my confession. Could it have been more? Now that I'm home, could Lincoln be trying to reach me to settle his unfinished business: to get my forgiveness. No, that was as silly as a dead tree granting death wishes. If I was going to be a doctor, I had to stop thinking like a lunatic.

"I'm confused," Evelyn admitted. "Is it one orb for each ghost? Cause if so, that's a lot of ghosts."

"Yeah, that's how it works," Hitch said.

Ghosts, that was preposterous. "If you believe in that kind of thing," I added.

Hitch corked an eyebrow "Wait, you don't? The whole reason you're home is because of some—"

I cut him off, "I said I was wrong about that; it was my guilt making me see things. Look at the film Hitch, you said it yourself, you only ever saw one orb on some top-secret film that when MIA. There's way too many. Look at all of them. It's a Christmas tree farm not a ghost farm."

That's right, there were hundreds of what Hitch dubbed spirit orbs. Lincoln was one person, thus potentially one orb. But Lincoln wasn't an orb, wasn't a spirit, I saw him in my mind's eye, not in real time. Hitch had helped me reign in my imagination, and I would do the same for him. I was sure what we were looking at was glare. I really should've minored in film.

Hitch put on the familiar air of a film student. "In *the biz*, we professionals call things like spirit orbs artifacts or white noise, and it's true nowhere in the history of film making has someone captured so many artifacts. But I'm not just anyone, I'm Charlie Hitch. It doesn't surprise me I accomplished something no one else has. The shame of it is that no one, not even my best friend, believes what they see. It's just like the human mind to come up with an explanation for the unexplainable."

I shook my head at him; it was as if Hitch and I swapped positions from this morning. I finally came to terms with reality and now Hitch was the one who thought something supernatural was going on at my family's tree farm.

"There's something else," he said, his voice taking on a serious tone. "The spirit orb I saw on the cut *Psycho* film, as I said, floated haphazardly, but these spirit orbs traveled in the same direction we were walking in as if they were following us."

"Did you see the spirit orbs while you were recording?" Evelyn asked.

Hitch shook his head. "Artifacts only show up on camera. That's what makes them so rare. You don't know what you have till postproduction."

"This is so interesting," Evelyn said, her eyes glued to the screen as the camera walked the dirt road of Lansbury Tree Farm. "Do we have sound? Maybe we can hear them say something."

"Yeah, we have sound," Hitch replied.

"No," I said firmly, not wanting Evelyn to hear my

confession to Lincoln's murder. I didn't care if Hitch's entire film class heard it, the world heard it, but not Evelyn Butler.

"No," Hitch corrected.

"Well, what is it, yes or no?" She glared at Hitch, her blue eyes deepening to slate.

"It's just that this is a top-secret film project."

"I'm not going to tell anyone. And besides, I thought you said you had a part for me."

She wrestled the TV controller from him, not that Hitch put up much of a fight, and turned on the volume.

The sound blared from the speakers just in time for her to catch the end of the video. "I wish Evelyn Butler would die."

The video ended and static filled the screen with a loud buzzing. Evelyn was fixated on my words, repeating them to herself like they were an incantation. I waited with bated breath for her to say something, my eyes never leaving her lips as she repeated what I said.

Hitch took the remote from Evelyn, she let him. He rewound the footage. This action seemed to stir her to life. She scooted over to have an unobstructed view of me from the other side of Hitch, a strawberry blush already creeping up her neck. "You wish I was dead?!"

"I didn't mean it."

She stood; her flush reaching her cheeks. She looked radiant when angry. "Well, you almost got your wish tonight didn't you Knox Lansbury?! You should have just let the tree fall on me like you let it fall on Lincoln!"

I also got to my feet, not sure what else to do. That was quite the accusation. Is that what people thought—that I let my brother die. Maybe I thought that too. Maybe that was why I decided to become a doctor. I wanted to save lives not take them.

My empty stomach churned; stomach bile found its way up

my esophagus. I thought I was going to be sick.

"Hate to break up your lover's quarrel, but you guys might want to see this?"

Evelyn and I peeled our eyes from each other and looked at the television. Hitch pushed play.

"What the . . ." I muttered.

"My thoughts exactly," Hitch said. "What the heck do you have going on at this farm?"

Our eyes were glued to the television as I made my confession. "I said it over and over again. I wish my brother were dead." As I spoke the little orbs that had followed us from the tree farm encircled me. As if on an invisible current they continued their journey toward the spider-web-like branches of the tree where they seemed to disappear through them.

Hitch fast forward to my similar wish for Evelyn. Again, we watched the spirit orbs move on their invisible current up and seemingly through the tree.

"The tree's like some supernatural conductor," I said, relying heavily on my science background. For whatever reason, the so-called spirit orbs seemed drawn to the tree as if by some unseen force. My mind went to natural magnets embedded in the Earth's crust as a logical explanation. I suppose it was possible one could be located on my family's tree farm, but it didn't explain the presence of the white orbs. At this point, I was open to them not being a product of glare. But what the heck did it all mean?

I sat back down on the floor, feeling lightheaded. I wished I never came home.

"I think it's more than that," Hitch said, replaying the segment again. "The orbs seem to respond to your voice," Hitch pointed out. "They're acting as a tuning fork matching the pattern of your voice."

He rewound the segment for the third time, being careful

not to let Evelyn hear any more of my confession than what was necessary. "Watch the orbs when you say, 'I wish my brother was dead'. The tree acts like an acoustic resonator, with every syllable an orb goes through the spider's nest."

"I don't see a spider's nest," Evelyn said. "Where do the orbs go after they disappear through the branches. And, if one of you say to the other side, I'm going to punch you."

With a grin, not able to resist, "I would say they went to the other side, but as far as the spider's nest, we're talking about the branches. As a child, the branches reminded me of spider webs."

She walked over and slugged my shoulder a tad bit harder than playful. "I can see how you think the branches look like spider webs, but I think they look more like dream catchers."

Hitch laughed, "The tree's a spirit catcher."

"You think so?" I asked Hitch earnestly.

"Yeah, don't you think so too," he said in a teasing voice. "You're the one who thinks the tree grants wishes after all."

"That would make it a wishing tree," Evelyn pointed out proudly, a broad smile plastered across her face.

"Or, if Knox is right, it's a killing tree."

As if just understanding the ramifications of what Hitch said, Evelyn spun on her heels and kicked me in the shin, hard. "You wished I died! You wished Lincoln dead, and he died! Oh my God and tonight a tree branch almost crushed me," she said scared, little red webs filling the corners of her eyes. "Am I going to die?! Is that tree really a killing tree?!"

"I didn't mean it."

And I didn't, not really. Evelyn was only a kid when she kissed Lincoln. My little brother was the most popular guy in school, could I really blame her for that. And even if I did, she didn't deserve to be flattened by a tree because of one kiss.

She pulled on my arm expectantly, forcing me to my feet.

"Knox, a tree branch almost crushed me tonight. I can't believe I'm believing all of this, but what if it's true? What if every time I go outside, I risk being crushed by a tree?!" Becoming enraged again, she locked my arm in her grip and squeezed. "You're going to go back to that tree, and you're going to wish for me to live a long and healthy life, do you hear me?!"

"I will. I promise."

She pulled me toward the front door. "I know you will because we're going right now!"

"That's a great idea," Hitch said. "I'll reshoot the walk to the tree. It'll be interesting to see if anything funny pops up on the footage."

Hitch ran up to the spare room to grab an extra battery pack.

I felt a little woozy as I put my father's Carhartt back on. "You should stay Evelyn. If trees are going to keep falling on you, it's best you stay in the house."

I wasn't sure what I believed at this point. Did I believe what I had believed since Lincoln's death, that my tree could indeed make my darkest desires come true or did I believe what I told myself that very morning, that it was all in my head. Either way, I didn't want Evelyn to come. My tree may hold mixed emotions for me now, but it was still my tree. My special spot, just from me. I didn't want to share it with her.

"Evelyn put on her coat and interlocked her arm with mine. "I'm coming. I need to make sure you do it right. Hopefully, if I'm attached to you, I'll be okay. That would mean if I die, you die and I don't think that's how wishes work. And if your wish does try to take us both out, you can push me out of the way again."

Her face became serious; and I realized she wasn't a child anymore, neither of us were. "I know I'm probably just overreacting, but I need to make sure. Tell me the truth, do you really believe the tree can grant wishes?"

I didn't get a chance to answer and I'm not sure if I knew the answer if I'd answer honestly.

"There's worse ways to die than with a beautiful woman on your arm," Hitch said, rejoining the room.

Evelyn smiled, clearly flattered. There was no denying it, Evelyn Butler was beautiful. I detested that seeing her had stirred up all these old, silly feelings for her. The kind of silly feelings only teenage boys get. After all these years, after what she'd done, how was it possible I still loved her?

* * *

We walked the dirt road through my family's tree farm.

"In another week this farm will be crawling with people," Evelyn told Hitch as he filmed. "Everyone in town comes to buy their Christmas tree from Lansbury Tree Farm."

"Everyone but Mr. Brentley," I added.

"That's true," she said with a smile, "everyone besides mean, old Mr. Brentley. It's hard to believe he's still alive. My mother said he was ancient when she was a kid."

A sparse chuckle escaped my lips. "You really make him out to be Elwood's Scrooge."

She laughed, "More like the Grinch locked away in his house surrounded by Christmas trees no one can buy."

"You're a mean one Mr. Brentley," I said in a sing-song tone to the tune of *You're a Mean One Mr. Grinch.*

Evelyn pulled me closer to her. "I'm really glad you're home. Your mother didn't say you were planning a visit."

There it was again, this mentioning of my mother. "It was a spur of the moment thing."

"Did you know Boris Koloff voiced the Grinch in the old cartoon special?" Hitch asked.

"Hmm?" We both muttered, pulled out of our conversation.

"You know, Boris Koloff, in my opinion the best Frankenstein."

"I didn't realize that was him," I said, recalling watching the short cartoon with Lincoln as kids."

"Yep, it's why it's a classic. But don't get confused. He didn't do the singing, just the voice acting."

"Good to know Hitch, thanks," I said, raising my eyebrows in false gratitude and smiling at Evelyn.

My smile was short lived, we'd made it to The Killing Tree. I preferred that name for my tree to Spirit Catcher or The Wishing Tree, despite the ominous meaning. This name embodied my idea of my family's tree farm. I recalled Shel Silverstein's *The Giving Tree*, a children's story about an apple tree that gave his little boy everything until nothing was left. Was that what my tree had done for me, had it given me exactly what I wanted? Had it glimpsed my soul and saw, if only for a split second, I *did* want my brother dead and Evelyn too?

I put my hand on my tree, to make a physical connection with it, hoping it would strengthen my wish. I couldn't believe just a few hours ago, after years of torment, I satisfied myself with thinking my wish and Lincoln's death were a coincidence and it was guilt that made me see his face in the tree. But here I was again, feeling there was something more—something beneath the surface.

I focused on Evelyn as I spoke. The light from Hitch's camera cast Evelyn's face in shadows, making her look like a dark angel. That scared me; it was as if Hitch was using movie magic to foreshadow the future.

"I made a wish today by accident. I DO NOT want Evelyn Butler to die. In fact, I wish for Evelyn Butler to live a long and healthy life."

The light from Hitch's camera seemed to explode, blinding my vision as my legs, like spaghetti, bent and gave way.

* * *

"Knox wake up."

I opened my eyes to see Lincoln standing next to me where I lay on the ground. I wrestled myself onto my elbows. "Lincoln," I said, barely audible, my breath filling the cold air like a coal furnace. "How are you here?" He looked just how he did the last time I saw him, down to the same T-shirt.

He glanced over his shoulder. "I can't stay. I need you to make me a promise, don't go Knox."

"What?"

"Promi—"

In the blink of an eye, Lincoln was gone and replaced with Evelyn Butler. She gripped my hand, "Knox, are you alright?"

I sat up confused. My body felt like ice. "What happened?" I scanned the trees for my brother.

"You fainted," Hitch said from behind me.

Craning my neck, I saw he was still filming.

Hitch gave me his best Cheshire Cat grin, patting the side of his camcorder. "Got the whole thing on film so you can watch it later. Epic fall. I mean epic!"

Evelyn's free hand brushed over the Band-Aid she'd placed earlier. We should get you back to the house. She turned to Hitch, "Can you put that thing down for one second and help me get him to his feet?!"

"Yes ma'am," he said, tucking his camcorder into his backpack.

Together, they helped me up. Hitch let me lean the majority of my weight on him until I got my bearings. Within a few minutes my brain fog cleared. I realized I must've imagined Lincoln, otherwise Evelyn and Hitch would've told me they saw him. I didn't want to worry them more, so I kept it to myself.

I felt my face. "My glasses."

"I have them," Evelyn said, handing them to me. "They're broken."

"I put them on, my vision fractured through the cracked lens. I had to take them right off, looking through a kaleidoscope was not going to help my pounding migraine.

* * *

I slumped onto the couch with my coat still on and cradled my head in my hands. As crappy as I felt, it was good to be home.

Evelyn unzipped her coat and sat next to me. "Want me to get something for your head? When I was looking for the peroxide, I saw Tylenol."

"Okay thanks," I said.

In a few minutes she was back in the living room with a glass of water and a bottle of Tylenol.

"You two ready?" Hitch asked, from his station in front of the television.

Evelyn paused from biting her nails. "Yeah, play it."

"I'll be dammed," Hitch said as we watched the spirit orbs glide along the trees at night. "This is just unheard of. No one at school is going to believe this is untouched film."

"What about when Knox made his wish?"

Hitch pushed fast forward.

In the video, like before, the spirit orbs followed us to my tree. But, unlike before, when I wished for Evelyn to live a long and healthy life, nothing happened. The spirit orbs stayed clustered around me and never ventured into the tree's spider-web-like branches.

"What does this mean?" Evelyn asked Hitch as if he had all the answers because he'd shot the footage.

"Um, I don't know, but if we're going under the assumption the tree can grant wishes, which I'm not sold on, then I would guess the tree didn't listen to Knox's latest wish. Lincoln's death wish, orbs disappear through big, dead, creepy tree, Evelyn's death wish, orbs disappear through big, dead, creepy tree, Evelyn's long, healthy life wish—diddly-squat."

"He doesn't know that's what it means," I told Evelyn, trying to calm her down. She was flushed again, an apple glow spreading across the bridge of her nose.

"You're right, I don't know. It's just a guess," Hitch said to me. "I believe the artifacts on the film are spirit orbs, what else could they be besides glare," he said, shooting me a glare of his own. "But the idea that a tree, no matter how strange and creepy it is, that can grant wishes, is well, just bonkers and I have a healthy imagination. Have to in my line of work. The tree branch falling at the winery tonight was a freak accident. So Evey, baby, you're safe, relax."

I didn't believe Hitch when he said he didn't think my tree could grant wishes. Maybe he thought that at first when I'd made my confession that morning, but I could tell by the way he twiddled his thumbs together anxiously, his mind was spinning. If he didn't think there was a possibility I had been right all along, he would've wished for something stupid to test the tree, like for a ham and cheese sandwich. But he didn't and I was sure he wouldn't now.

I was back to my original thought about my tree, that somehow it did fulfill my wish for Lincoln to die. It didn't matter that there was no logical explanation for it, sometimes things just couldn't be explained. Even in the sciences, this phenomenon happened. I had been going back and forth so much, I felt like I gave myself mental whiplash, but I knew the truth now. I felt it. I felt it when I put my hand on its rough bark, the dead tree was alive.

"How do we know for sure I'm safe?" Evelyn asked.

Hitch shrugged, "I guess we have to wait and see."

She threw a couch pillow at him. "Wait and see?! I could be dead!"

"Don't be mad at me, I'm not the one who made the wish."

Hitch looked to me for answers. I had none. I made a mistake and now Evelyn Butler was going to die. But I couldn't tell her that. I should've been furious with Hitch for having me believe it was the guilt making me see things, but this was on me. I should've trusted my instinct. A good doctor always does, even a future one.

Evelyn broke the silence. "Why don't we ask Mr. Brentley?"

"Why him?" I asked.

"The tree's technically on his property."

"You know he doesn't like visitors, and I don't see how he could help."

"Listen, the two of you," she said, pointing at us. "I'm not going to wait around for a tree to fall on me. The fact is this: Knox wished for me to die and tonight a tree branch almost crushed me to death. That's all the evidence I need. Something strange is going on and it has something to do with that huge, dead tree." She honed in on me. "I don't care if you don't know how going to Mr. Brentley can help. It's a start. Maybe he knows about the tree or at the very least he can tell us what type of tree it is, and we can do our own research from there. This is my life. I'm not taking any chances."

Hitch chimed in "And if I film on his side of the fence we can find out where the spirit orbs are going. I'm not sure how that will help Evelyn, but any little clue will help us figure out why this tree supposedly accepts death wishes."

I had to do something to stop what I set in motion; I knew that. Just the thought of being the reason Evelyn dies had already twisted a cannon-ball-size knot in my stomach. Hitch may not believe in my wish, but Evelyn did, and I did. Maybe Evelyn was right, and Mr. Brentley could set us on the right track. What else could we do? My head was thumping like it had its own heartbeat. I couldn't think straight. At the moment, I had no better idea. "Okay, fine, we'll go to Mr. Brentley."

CHAPTER FIVE
Mr. Brentley's House

I was against going to Mr. Brentley's on the principle disturbing him was pointless but to go to his house close to 9 p.m. seemed anything but irreprehensible. Evelyn and Hitch wouldn't wait till tomorrow, and I was outnumbered. I didn't want Evelyn to doubt I cared, so I had no choice but to go along.

It wasn't a far walk to Mr. Brentley's house. We just had to go left where we would have gone right to get to The Killing Tree. Nevertheless, the walk felt a lot longer thanks to the drop in temperature. I yanked the collar of my coat up, wishing I'd remembered to grab my scarf.

The grinning moon was fully visible in the sky. Not one cloud spoiled the starry night. It would have been a dream come true to walk under a sky like that with Evelyn Butler, but under the threat of her pending doom I couldn't enjoy it.

I wished my head would stop buzzing so I could think. The day had blown by with everything happening at warp speed. I needed time to analyze the situation. The last four years had left my mind grounded in science, but science wasn't going to solve this. I needed to start thinking like, I don't know, a kid again. Reverse engineer my mind and start thinking how I did when I was in high school, when I first realized something was off with the tree. No—

that wasn't right, it started way before that. I knew it when I first saw it. But how and why? That's what I needed to figure out, if I was to help Evelyn. What about the tree first drew me to it? Why did I decide it was *my* tree? What made me talk to it? What made me share with it my most inner desires? And perhaps, the most interesting thing about my tree was that I kept it a secret from my parents and from Lincoln. Why did I feel compelled to do that?

Hitch was the first person I ever showed my tree to. Evelyn, of course, now also knew about it. But I hadn't wanted to share it with them. I convinced myself my confession had to be in front of my tree, so by default, Hitch had to be there. Having him there and then bringing him and Evelyn back to my secret spot made me feel like I was betraying an old friend. What was it about that big, dead tree that made me feel that way?

The time for introspection was over, we made our way into Mr. Brentley's front yard. Only one light was on. The light in question was in the highest room, most likely an attic, and was left on accidentally.

"He must be asleep," I said.

"No," Hitch countered, "listen, do you hear that?"

I closed my eyes to focus on the sound. Lincoln's face popped into my mind. He blinked and was about to open his eyes when mine flew open, my breathing quickening to a gallop. I couldn't hear anything over my own heartbeat.

"I hear it," Evelyn said. "There're so many voices . . . like he's having a party."

"With the lights off?" I asked, dumbfounded. I too could hear the voices as we approached the porch. Evelyn was right, it sounded like he was holding a large gathering. The sound buzzing from the home, a cacophony of voices.

"He's a kinky old man," Hitch said with a laugh as we walked up the steps to the old, brick manor home. He had his camera out, capturing a panoramic view.

Even at night, Mr. Brentley's house was impressive. It had three rows of large windows all clad with heavy, wood shutters not including the copper encrusted ocular window of the attic, to which the left on light shone out to the porch. It reminded me of a great cyclops eye. The open porch ran the expanse of the house culminating at each end with a brick chimney. Two massive corbels formed a portico over the front door, casting the door in complete darkness.

I rang the doorbell, a sweet chime that reminded me of a lullaby I hadn't heard since I was a toddler filled the night's air. Before I pulled my finger from the doorbell, the house came alive. Every light in the large home lit in unison.

"Creepy," Hitch said, extending the word. He wasn't creeped out, he was excited. He had on his Cheshire Cat grin that rivaled the moon.

We didn't have to wait long for the proprietor of the home. A few moments after the lights flashed on, the front door opened a crack. A thin trail of light spilled out into the darkness, pouring over my face. Mr. Brentley, with the aid of a cane, peered out his front door. Thick rimmed glasses dulled his green eyes. A gray beard masked his gaunt face and razor thin lips.

"Hi, Mr. Brentley," I said, speaking for the group. "I'm not sure if you remember me but it's Knox Lansbury from next door. I hope I'm not bothering you."

At my name, he opened the door fully. He looked pleased to see me, that was before he noticed I wasn't alone. He pointed at Hitch. "No cameras," he said it in such a tone, Hitch didn't even use his, 'I'm a film student' line.

Mr. Brentley watched Hitch with the jade eyes of a hawk behind his glasses. As Hitch put his camera away, I spoke up. "I was hoping we could talk to you."

"I would accommodate your request Knox, owing to the respect I have for your mother, but I was just getting ready to go to bed."

Hitch peaked into the house, making sure not to step over the threshold. "You're not having a party?"

"Is this an interview?" Mr. Brentley asked back, coldly.

"No, I'm just inquisitive. I'm a film student."

There it was, the film student line. Mr. Brentley didn't seem to care.

"If you must know, I'm spending the evening as I spend every evening—alone."

"I'm sorry," I said, realizing I started this whole thing off on the wrong foot. Maybe Mr. Brentley would be a little more accommodating if I introduced the strangers standing at his doorstep to him. "Mr. Brentley let me introduce my friends to you. This is—"

"Charles Hitchcock," he said, finishing my sentence.

"How did you know my name?" Hitch asked like an accusation.

I made a downward motion with my hand, signaling for Hitch to relax.

"I know everything that goes on in my town."

His eyes glanced over Evelyn slowly, almost as if he was studying her. "And this is Ms. Evelyn Butler. I'm glad to see you're well after what happened at the Vinter Wonderland attraction."

Evelyn squeezed my arm.

With a nod, Mr. Brentley went to close the door. After all the trouble, I wasn't going to leave empty-handed. I put my foot out, impeding the door from closing. "There's a tree on your property we need information about."

Mr. Brentley took off his glasses and cleaned them with a small cloth he pulled from his sweater vest pocket. "I don't see why this can't wait till tomorrow; even so, all the trees on my estate are the same variety of Fir trees as the trees on your family's farm Knox."

"You're mistaken Mr. Brentley, I'm not talking about the Christmas trees, the tree I'm talking about is different." I stretched my hands over my head, trying to think of a way to describe it. "It's huge and dead. It borders the property line on your side. Do you know the one I'm talking about?"

"I can't say I do," he said coolly. "Now if you don't mind, I'm very tired. He tapped my boot with the tip of his cane.

"Of course," I said, "I'm sorry, but before you go can we have permission to explore your tree farm?"

His answer came swiftly and in the same firm voice he had used with Hitch earlier. "I can't grant you permission."

"Why not?" Evelyn asked, hiding part of her face behind my back.

"If I let you three on my land others will catch wind of it and soon my beautiful trees will be assigned to the executioner. They will find themselves cut down and stuffed into corners dressed in popcorn and cranberries like a corpse in a nice shirt and tie."

It unnerved me to hear Mr. Brentley talk about the trees in terms I had earlier related to Hitch. Judging by Hitch's twisted up face, it also disturbed him. I wasn't sure if it was from the likely concussion or fainting, but my legs suddenly felt wobbly under my weight.

"Good night, Knox," he said, with another tap on my boot with his cane.

I removed my foot, and the door shut, once again shrouding the front door in darkness.

"That man scares me," Evelyn whispered. "How did he know who I was and what happened tonight?"

It dawned on me, tonight was the first time Evelyn met Mr.

Brentley and the same went for Hitch. He shouldn't have known them, but he did. I shrugged my shoulders. It was the only answer I had for her. My brain felt like pudding as I with Evelyn, still linked to my arm, stepped off the porch.

"Well," Hitch said, his camera making a reappearance, "now I'm definitely checking out his tree farm."

"You heard him," I said, my liquefied brain sloshing around in pain.

"I did," Hitch admitted. "That's why we're going to wait for him to go to bed before we jump the fence."

I groaned. "Fine, we jump the fence. But not tonight. He'll be expecting something like that."

"What makes you think that?" Hitch asked.

I inclined my head back toward the house. Mr. Brentley's thin frame was visible in the first window to the right of the front door. All of the lights were still on in the house. He wasn't going to bed, not now.

"He's watching us, and I don't doubt he'll call the police. With the amount of 'No Trespassing' signs he has posted, you won't be able to talk your way out of getting booked.

It was Hitch who groaned now. "I'm not eager to get arrested. Alfred Hitchcock was afraid of cops and so am I. Let's check out the new footage and come back tomorrow."

* * *

I wanted nothing more than to plop down on the living room couch, but when we came through the front door my parents were cozied up on the couch watching the Hallmark channel. That was one thing I didn't miss about the holidays with my parents—watching the Hallmark Christmas countdown.

My mother hopped up to greet me. "We must have just missed you at the winery," she said, planting a kiss on my cheek. She noticed the Band-Aid. "Knox, what happened?" She looked to my father, "See David, I told you something happened." She turned back to me, sandwiching my face between her hands to examine me for other injuries. "I told your father something happened. When I saw the peroxide on the table, I feared the worst."

I pulled the Band-Aid off. "Mom it's nothing. I tripped on the steps. Can you believe it?!"

"I can," my father said from the couch.

"Don't mind your father, he's in one of his moods."

I didn't look my father's way. I wouldn't give him the satisfaction.

Hitch really knew how to oversell a story. "Knox is a real klutz sometimes. He'd find a way to hurt himself in a padded room."

I guess that was better than telling my mom I almost got crushed by a tree than fainted.

"Where's your glasses?" My mother asked, no doubt accustomed to seeing me always wearing them.

"They broke, but don't worry Mom, I have another pair in my room."

I tugged Evelyn's coat. "Mom, you remember Evelyn Butler from school, don't you?"

She smiled politely, "Of course. Evelyn, what a nice surprise."

"Hi Mrs. Lansbury. Your home looks so nice and festive. I love how you decorated the tree."

"Thank you dear. Now, have you kids eaten yet? I made some homemade pizza," she offered, gesturing to the pizza on the coffee table.

"Starving," Hitch said, throwing off his coat and helping himself to a slice. "To quote the great Alfred Hitchcock: *Man does not live by murder alone. He needs affection, approval, encouragement and, occasionally, a hearty meal.*"

I hung up my coat and Evelyn's while she took a slice of pizza. "Thanks Mrs. Lansbury."

"So uh, do you guys stay up late?" Hitch asked, shielding his mouth with his hand as he chewed.

"Pretty late," my father answered, his eyes on the television.

Hitch gave me a wink and smiled, meant to be a code for something. "Good, hopefully you'll still be up after we drop Evelyn off."

Understood—he wanted use of a television and that meant it was time to go to Evelyn's.

"You're not staying for the movie Knox? It's a good one," my mom said in her disappointed voice. That tone usually bent my will to hers, but not tonight.

"Sorry Mom, tomorrow. I promise."

I glanced to Hitch and Evelyn. "I'll just grab my glasses while you guys get something to eat."

I made a beeline for the staircase. I knew I should eat something. Hitch nailed it when he said starving, but I was also nauseous. What a horrible way to feel. I was sure it was just the side effect of my concussion, but I knew if I ate pizza, I would be tossing up pizza.

I entered my room and went to the luggage I'd left open on my bed. I found my glasses case and went to the mirror on the wall. It still had Dragon Ball Z stickers all over it. I donned my spare pair of glasses. The frames were thicker than my favorite pair. I nibbled my bottom lip worried my glasses made me look dorky. Who was I kidding, I was and am dorky, but the last thing I wanted was to look it in front of Evelyn Butler. These frames had to be the pinnacle of the 'science stuff' Hitch warned me about.

I took my glasses off and placed them back in their case. I always thought my green eyes were more vibrant without glasses, but I couldn't stand wearing contacts.

I ran my hand over the cut on the side of my temple. Evelyn was right, it wasn't deep, but the skin along it was bruised. It was the sickly sallow pallor a bruise takes on before it becomes the iconic black and blue. It looked like my second inclination, that it was caused by a clash of heads, was right on the money.

I slid my glasses case into my jean pocket and went into the hall. The room next to mine was Lincoln's. I let myself in. I didn't want to go downstairs right away and risk my mother trying to force feed me.

My mom left Lincoln's room, like mine, a time capsule. Nothing had changed. Nothing was moved. On the shelf next to his bed were his trophies from track, soccer, and football. I sat on his made bed, smoothing out the covers. From his window, I could see the edge of our property. I could see Mr. Brentley's attic light was still on, along with all of the others.

I closed my eyes, taking a deep breath, letting the air sit in my lungs before I released it slowly. There Lincoln was, his eyes wide open in death, blood dripping into them from the corners. I felt cold without noticing a change in the room temperature. I heard Lincoln's voice in my head. "Don't go Knox."

I fought against instinct to open my eyes. I spoke in a whisper, my chest heaving. "Lincoln, if you're there, I forgive you. Please move on."

"What are you doing in here?" My mother asked from the door.

Startled at hearing my mother's voice, my eyes flew open. "Sorry, I was just . . ."

She came in and sat beside me. "It's okay. I come in here sometimes to think too."

She squeezed my hand tenderly, in the way only a mother can. "It's okay to miss him."

I didn't want to talk about Lincoln. I couldn't until I sorted out all the things in my head. "Why didn't you tell me Evelyn asked about me?"

"Evelyn Butler," my mother said, with a shake of her head. "I'd rather you not hang around that girl. She's not for you Knox, she's not going places like you are. She's working as a waitress at Chubby's until she can catch her free ride. Her mother was the same way. The apple doesn't fall far from the tree."

I could've done without the lecture and the tree idiom.

"I don't mean to meddle in your affairs, Evelyn seems nice enough but after the trouble she caused between Lincoln and you, well it's best you just don't see her again."

"You know about that?" I asked, not wanting to tell her something she didn't actually know.

"Lincoln told me the night it happened. He left the prom early to look for you."

"I didn't know."

She squeezed my hand tighter, her grip hurting my hand. "Did you two make up before it happened."

I looked into my mother's blue eyes and lied. "Yes Mom, we made up. When Lincoln died, we were good, as we always were." She hugged me like a vice, her hands wrapping around me as if she was never going to let me go. "Thank God. I always prayed you did but was too scared to ask you all these years." I felt her warm tears penetrate my shirt. I did my best to bite back my own.

CHAPTER SIX
Evelyn Butler's House

We watched the footage taken outside of Mr. Brentley's house close to ten times. Each time Hitch pointed out the same things: how the spirit orbs were visible when the house lights were off and how they disappeared when they came on, the strange look in Mr. Brentley's green eyes, and the orbs visible behind the fence I wouldn't let him jump over.

"This whole thing has really freaked me out," Evelyn said, drawing the throw around her shoulders tighter. "At least we can all agree the spirit orbs are spirit orbs at least. The new footage proves it. The orbs wouldn't have disappeared when Mr. Brentley turned on the lights if it was glare or a camera malfunction."

It's funny, I wasn't sold on the white orbs being spirit orbs and thought my tree granted death wishes and Hitch was of the opposite thinking, the white orbs absolutely being spirit orbs and not sold on the wishing power of my tree. But I had to agree with Evelyn, there was nothing wrong with Hitch's camera and whatever the orbs were, they weren't glare. If there was a connection between my tree and the orbs, I couldn't imagine what it would be.

Hitch patted his camera like it was a faithful dog. "I didn't think it was my camera, it being new and state of the art."

"I just hope that if all this wishing tree business is real,

Knox's last wish worked. I just wish we knew," Evelyn said. "Urgh, No more wishing."

"It did," I said from the sofa where I sat with Hitch. "It had to." There was nothing saying it didn't. Would it kill us to think positively?! We could be worrying for no reason. We could have already solved the problem with a counter wish. Who cares what the strange white orbs did in the video?! There's no correlation to prove they have anything to do with the wishing. Lincoln was already dead when Hitch filmed me, so it didn't matter what the orbs did when I wished for Evelyn to die. I wish Hitch hadn't put the idea in her head. I hated to see her upset.

Evelyn got up from the armrest of the sofa and rubbed her hands over her arms. Her trailer was drafty. I noticed duct tape on the front window when we walked in, but it was too cold in there to be coming just from that. Evelyn had plugged in some space heaters when we first got there. It helped a little.

As Hitch hooked his camcorder up to the television, she'd attempted to straighten up but no amount of straightening up could cover up the different flooring under our feet or the holes in the small sofa. I had no idea Evelyn lived like this. I'd never been to her house, and she always seemed well-dressed at school, even if she wasn't in brand-name clothing.

An old trunk served as a coffee table. A small, artificial Christmas tree, the kind you find at the Dollar Tree, sat centered on it. The foot-tall tree had little ornaments adorning it, that I assumed were also purchased from the dollar store. It was the only tree in her house. She had told Hitch everyone in town got their Christmas tree from Lansbury Tree Farm. It appeared, everyone but Mr. Brentley and the Butlers. I never realized it before. I had always seen her at the farm, but she was there with friends helping them pick out their Christmas tree. Evelyn never came with her mother to get their own.

She stood in front of the TV and faced Hitch and me on the sofa. "I guess there's nothing else we can do till tomorrow, but um, do you think you guys could spend the night? I don't want to be alone, and my mom works the graveyard shift at the super Walmart in Glassco and won't be home until 9 a.m."

"Yeah," I said, without hesitation, "we can stay."

"One problem," Hitch pointed out, covering himself with the throw Evelyn had abandoned. "We both have bad backs. I hope you have another couch or one of us is going to have to room with you."

I didn't have a bad back nor did Hitch. He shot me a wink.

"Someone can have my bed. I can sleep on the floor."

"No need for that," Hitch chirped. "Knox is skinny. You two take your bed. I'll take the couch but be a doll and get me a pillow and another blanket."

"I can sleep on the floor," I insisted.

"Don't be silly, you have a bad back. We can sleep head to toe if you feel weird about it."

* * *

I stood in Evelyn's room in awe as she took Hitch a pillow and some more blankets. I had never been in a girl's room before. I was sure my mouth was hanging open like a dog with its head out the window on a car ride. I felt like I stepped into another world. Where the rest of the trailer seemed in disrepair, Evelyn's room looked like a Lisa Frank unicorn vomited all over it. Every inch of her walls were covered with posters, magazine clippings, and stickers. I noticed her bras hanging on the back of the door, and instantly felt dizzy. There were so many and in so many different colors.

"You feeling any better?" Evelyn asked, coming back into the room.

I jerked my head away from the bras. "Yeah," I said, my

hand instinctively going to my head. "My splitting headache is now just a dull one."

She had changed into her pajamas. The top was red with a silkscreen of the gingerbread man from the movie *Shrek*. The pants, also red, had mini gingerbread men all over them in different sizes and directions. Red was her color. I wondered if she knew that.

"Good, that means you're on the mend. Do you want to borrow a pair of pajama pants? I hate sleeping in jeans."

"Um, yeah, that would be great."

She handed me a pair of men's plaid pants that she pulled from the top drawer of her dresser. I wondered if they were her boyfriend's.

"Guy pants are always the most comfortable," she said as if she read my mind.

I put my glasses on her dresser before I turned from her to trade my jeans for the pants. Luckily, she wore her PJ's big, they fit me perfectly. I climbed into Evelyn's bed, my head resting at the foot of the bed. She tossed me a stuffed penguin to use as a pillow.

"Sorry, I only have two pillows, and Hitch got the other one."

"No worries, I like penguins," I said, putting it under my head.

"Night Knox. If I accidently kick you in the middle of the night, sorry."

"Apology accepted."

She reached over and shut off the old lamp on her nightstand.

I was exhausted. I was happy to finally be lying down even if my pillow was a stuffed penguin. And on top of that, I was in Evelyn Butler's bed. Evelyn Butler, my childhood crush—the first girl I ever loved. I wished I could've savored the moment longer, but my eyelids felt like they were made of lead.

I was just about to drift off when I felt Evelyn's foot brush against my outer thigh. I was thinking this was the accidental kicking she'd apologize for, but then her big toe played with the button that closed my fly. I did everything I could to remain calm, but it was impossible. It was blissful torture. I didn't want her to stop. But then she did, and the real torture started. My heart pounded in my chest like a drum. I wished it would be quiet, I desperately wanted to listen for a sign Evelyn was still awake and that her foot was going to find my groin again.

As if she read my mind for the second time that night, she stirred, pushing the covers off of us before climbing on top of me. She kissed me, her curls falling around her face like a dark halo. I kissed her back, not letting our mouths separate. She pulled down my pajama pants then hers. While her body rose and fell against mine, nothing mattered. There was no Hitch in the living room, no worried mother, no looming death wish, no dead brother—there was just Evelyn Butler. I pulled her closer, trying to hold on to the perfect moment, but soon it all seeped back in: my strange tree, the strange white orbs, Evelyn's strange near death experience, Lincoln's strange death, Mr. Brentley and his strange house.

Evelyn rolled off of me. We remained quiet. After a few moments, she took my hand in hers. I still couldn't speak. I was breathing louder than normal. I wasn't sure if I breathed like that the whole time, but now I couldn't help but notice. It seemed ear-splitting in the quiet room.

"Knox, are you okay?"

My throat was dry. My head pounded as all the blood rushed back to it. "Why did you do that?"

I shouldn't question a good thing, but it was in my nature. Evelyn had just told me a few hours ago she used me to get to Lincoln, why all of a sudden, after all these years, did she want to sleep with dorky, old me? My mother's warning about Evelyn looking for her free ride replayed in my head.

She talked in a whisper, still grasping my hand. "Why? — Because you saved my life."

I sat up, pulling my hand from hers and yanking my pants up. "So, it was payment."

She sidled up to me. "Don't say it like that. I wanted to and I thought you did too."

I'm self-destructive. I know that now. I just couldn't leave it dead and buried. Just as Evelyn Butler was the first girl I loved; she was the first girl I hated. She was the girl who came between my brother and me. Being home had stirred up all of my old feelings and I couldn't hide from them like I'd done in California.

"And if Lincoln was alive, you wouldn't have given me five minutes of your time. You said so yourself, you went with me to prom to be near him."

She rubbed her face against my arm. "That was a long time ago."

"Yeah, it was, and now he's dead and I'm your ticket out of this crummy little town and shit life you built for yourself."

Tears fell before I finished my sentence. She rushed out of the room. I heard the front door slam.

I ran after her furious with myself. I finally got Evelyn Butler to like me, even if it was only because Lincoln was out of the picture. I guess I wasn't over their kiss, no matter how long ago it was. I now understood that in the heat of the moment, I meant every word of it when I wished Lincoln and Evelyn dead. I had to come to terms with that, just like I had to accept that I wasn't Evelyn's first choice.

I went outside and scanned the yard. The temperature had plummeted. The ground was covered in a heavy frost that sparkled like white diamonds under the outside floodlight.

I had only taken the time to slip on my boots, leaving my coat inside as Hitch was using it as a second pillow. I was just about to yell for Evelyn when I noticed she was sitting in the back seat of the Dodge.

I jogged over to my mom's car and got in. She wiped her tears with her coat sleeve. How could I ever wish Evelyn dead and mean it?

"Evelyn," I said, touching her arm. She recoiled. I kept my hands to myself. "I'm sorry for what I said. You're right, it was a long time ago and I had no business bringing it up like I did."

She looked out the window, refusing to look at me. "No you're not. You meant everything you said. About payment, about your brother, about you thinking I'm some blood sucking leech trying to latch onto you for substance."

She pawed at her face again with her sleeve. "I was happy for you when your mom told me you got into Stanford Med. I didn't think seeing you tonight was my ticket out of Elwood. That's not why I came over to say hi. When I heard my name and spotted you, I thought this is someone I wronged for no good reason, and I should apologize. And then you saved my life, and I don't know. I'm not trying to latch on to you. I didn't sleep with you because of that." She sniffled. "A one-night stand is what it is, you don't have to read into it. I'm on birth control, so you don't have to worry about me trapping you."

She finally faced me. Tears streamed from her blue eyes like waterfalls, it was beautiful and terrifying to watch. "I'm sorry about what happened between your brother and me and you and your brother because of me. I deserve your wish. I was horrible to you. I'm sorry. I can't say it enough. If I could go back in time, I never would have hurt you like that. You've always been nice to me Knox, even when I didn't deserve it. Can you forgive me?"

I froze. It was the same thing Lincoln had asked of me. Here was my chance to accept her apology, if I wanted. But, if I did, I had to let it go and move on. I couldn't have a future with Evelyn if I was stuck in the past.

I reached for her hand, she let me hold it. "Yes Evelyn, I forgive you. Now come on, let's get inside."

We went back to her room, sneaking past Hitch who was still sound asleep on the sofa. Evelyn took off her winter coat and tossed it on her desk chair. I climbed into her bed. Reaching for her hand, I pulled her down next to me, wrapping my arms around her and pressing a kiss to the side of her beautiful face. "I'm sorry," I whispered in her ear. She turned and our lips met. And just like that, I was wholly head over heels in love with Evelyn Butler for the second time.

CHAPTER SEVEN
Cookies and Milk

"Mrs. Butler told me something very interesting as we waited for you two love birds to wake up," Hitch said as we got into the Dodge in the morning.

Evelyn pulled back the living room curtain and waved.

I smiled, throwing the car in reverse.

"Ah, *parting is such sweet sorrow*," Hitch said, batting his eyelashes and waving regally to Evelyn from the passenger side window. "*Romeo and Juliet*," the late, great William Shakespeare."

"Hey! You didn't give me a chance to guess the quote," I said as I backed out of Evelyn's driveway, looking to the trailer for one last glimpse of her. "I actually knew that one. I read it in high school."

"I'm sure you did Romeo."

With an elbow to my side, "Am I a good friend or what?"

"The very best," I said, meaning it.

"So how was last night?"

"I'm not answering any of those types of questions," I said with a grin that I was sure was easy to read. "You were saying Mrs. Butler said something interesting."

Hitch reclined his seat. "Oh yeah that! She told me that mean, old Mr. Brentley is a real piece of work. She said when

Evelyn's father died, and she fell on hard times, she went to Mr. Brentley asking for more time to come up with rent.

"Let me guess. He said humbug and refused. And later that night he was visited by three ghosts."

"That's too easy Knox. You're referring to the immortal *A Christmas Carol* by the never duplicated Charles Dickens. And no, she said Mr. Brentley told her he could give her more time to come up with rent for a price."

My eyes flashed in his direction when he didn't tell me what the price was, forcing me to ask. "For what price, Hitch?"

"What does every sleazy, old man want?"

My eyes darted his way again. "Sex?" Now that I experienced it, I'd imagine it was what any man would want, not that they had the right to barter for it like that.

"Bingo. She refused and stormed out. Apparently, Mrs. Butler used to be a knockout. Her words, not mine. The important part of her story was that other people had had similar experiences with him."

"That's very interesting Hitch. I guess he's just a *squeezing, wrenching, grasping, scraping, clutching, covetous, old sinner,*" I said, quoting *A Christmas Carol.*

"What *I* found interesting is that he literally owns the whole town, every property and business except one. Do you know what property that is?"

"My family's."

Hitch's eyes bulged from their sockets, like Arnold Schwarzenegger's at the end of *Total Recall.* A feat I'm sure Hitch would've been proud of if he could've seen himself. "So, you do know?!

"By *owns the whole town,* if you mean everyone pays rent to Mr. Brentley—then yes, I know. I told you that much yesterday. And as far as my family's farm is concerned, my mother had enough money to buy our property outright when she and my father moved into town. If you hadn't noticed, Elwood isn't exactly the Hamptons."

"Oh okay, thanks for straightening that out," he said mockingly. "Mrs. Butler said that when the Lansburys moved to Elwood, Mr. Brentley *gave* them the piece of property right next to his. I guess she forgot to mention your mom was independently wealthy and bought it outright."

I pulled into my parent's driveway next to my father's Ford pickup, my eyes glazing over my family's beautiful log cabin. "I don't like what you're insinuating."

"I'm not insinuating anything," he said palms up in a sign of innocence. "Your minx of a mother probably just finished stitching the holes in your socks and is preparing to pray the Rosary."

"That Mrs. Butler sure left an impression on you, "I said disgusted, letting my slight country accent shine. "I suppose it's more fun to listen to her gossip than to trust the woman who's opened her home to you."

"And birthed my best friend," Hitch added. "Lighten up, Knox. I was just trying to prove the point that Mr. Brentley is sneaky, and we should jump his fence, that's all. Your mom is awesome. So awesome that if she and your dad ever split you can call me Papa. You know I have a thing for bombshell blondes even when they're double my age. After all, with age comes experience."

I got out of the Dodge, slamming the door.

"I said I'd jump the fence with you already. You don't have to keep trying to convince me. And please don't talk about having the hots for my mom, it's creepy and Mr. Brentley's really not that bad. Evelyn and her mother may think of him as mean, old Mr. Brentley but I don't remember him that way."

"Really?" Hitch said, following me to my front door. "What I saw last night was mean among other things."

"That's why I didn't want to go to see him last night. I had enough good sense to know dropping by an elderly man's home unexpected, and at night, is rude. I'm not sure how you and Evelyn expected him to act. If we'd waited till today to go, like I had suggested, he probably would have been a little warmer and who knows, gave us permission to walk his property."

"Maybe," Hitch admitted with a shrug.

"I remember him being nice. Every year around Christmas my mother bakes him cookies and drops them off. One year I went. I was probably six, I don't remember if Lincoln was with us . . . That's right, it was only my mother and me."

Hitch stopped me from opening the front door. "That's our ticket in."

"What is?"

"You have your mom bake some cookies, then you go with her to Mr. Brentley's to drop them off while I snoop around in his yard."

"She doesn't drop them off till closer to Christmas."

"I'm sure you can talk her into dropping them off early. A little mother-son baking day would make your visit complete." He pushed the front door open. "Let's ask her."

* * *

Mr. Brentley opened the door to see my mother and me holding out a large tin of cookies. He smiled and ushered us in. A sense of déjà vu washed over me. All the furniture in the house was covered with white sheets to protect it from dust. The house appeared to have been winterized as if no one was expected to come back until the warm weather hit. But Mr. Brentley's home was not a summer home. It was made for winter with its two chimneys and evergreen views.

I recalled that as a child the house had looked the same, sheets covered everything, even the paintings on the walls.

As a boy, at first, I thought the sheets were ghosts. I was terrified until Mr. Brentley lifted them up to show me what was hiding underneath. "Things are not always what they seem Knox," he had said to me with a kind smile before I followed him into the kitchen with my mother.

We now followed Mr. Brentley into his kitchen, taking the same route we did all those years ago. I couldn't resist pulling up a sheet that, in fact, looked like a ghost. Underneath was a globe on a wooden stand. I smiled at my foolishness. But in fairness, the house would've looked haunted to anyone, with its white mounds rising from the ground and looming shadows moving along the drapes thanks to the heating registers in the floor.

Just like the first time I came to Mr. Brentley's house, he opened the tin of cookies from my mother and placed them in front of me. "Have all you like."

"I had eaten more than a few when we were baking and was cookied out. However, I didn't want to be rude after last night, so I plucked from the tin the smallest chocolate chip cookie I could spot. "Thank you."

He poured me a glass of milk without me asking. "I recall you like to dunk your cookies in milk."

I smiled. "Yeah, that's right."

He seemed delighted to have my mother and me at his house. His step seemed lighter, like his cane was more for pomp than necessity. His face didn't seem vexed in the day light, but joyful. He was exactly how I remembered him.

"I believe the last time you were here you wished to eat them all," Mr. Brentley reminisced.

My mother laughed. "He did say that." She tousled my hair like I was still a boy. "Knox has always had a sweet tooth. Isn't that right honey?"

I nodded, dunking my cookie in the milk.

I had said that. I had forgotten all about it. When Mr. Brentley put the tin of cookies in front of me as a boy, my eyes lit up like two Christmas trees and I said: "I wish I could eat them all."

Mr. Brentley had responded in the same manner as he did moments ago: "Have all you like."

I don't recall my mom finding it funny then. She was angry that he gave me permission to eat my fill of cookies. I remember her giving Mr. Brentley the same face she gave me when I did something wrong, but she didn't contradict him. While she and Mr. Brentley went into the other room to talk, I think that's what they were doing—yes, they were talking, I devoured cookie after cookie until I got a terrible stomachache.

I remember them coming back into the kitchen, Mr. Brentley's line of gray teeth peeking out of his beard as he smiled at the six-year-old me. He leaned down and whispered in my ear: "You have learned a very important lesson today, Knox. Be careful what you wish for."

A chill ran through my body that left my hands trembling. I let the rest of my cookie sink to the bottom of my glass. I wanted to leave. I was glad Evelyn was at work. I didn't want her to get dragged into this any more than she had to be.

At the minimum, I had convinced Hitch that jumping a who knows how tall fence with barbed wire crowning it was a bad idea. I, instead, gave him the keys to the Dodge and sent him to Mr. Henderson's Hardware store on Main to buy bolt cutters. I figured if we cut the chain link fence where The Killing Tree had grown into it, we'd be able to slip through without anyone noticing.

I still didn't know what Hitch expected to find on Mr. Brentley's property. I suppose he was looking for a logical explanation for the white orbs. His fixation was on them. At this point, I hoped there was a connection between my tree and their spirit orbs and whatever we found on the other side of the fence could help Evelyn.

My phone went off. I pulled it from my sweater. It was Evelyn. I excused myself and walked into the sheet covered living room.

"Hi," I said into the phone, trying not to sound too eager. I had been hoping she would text me all morning and afternoon. I was thrilled to get a call.

"Knox," she said in a shaky voice.

My pulse surged. "What's wrong?"

"Can you pick me up? I'm at the hospital."

"On my way."

I popped my head into Mr. Brentley's kitchen to let him and my mother know I had to leave. Before I could speak, Mr. Brentley tapped on my glass of milk ladened with cookie chunks, "Looks like you finally learned your lesson."

His words struck a chord in my heart. I didn't think he was talking about cookies anymore. "I, uh, have to run."

CHAPTER EIGHT
A Warning

Evelyn was sitting with her arm in a sling when we walked into the Emergency Room waiting room. I rushed to her, wanting to throw my arms around her, but hesitated awkwardly in mid hug. Were we something now? Last night seemed like years ago. Evelyn stood up to finish the hug, ending it with a soft kiss on my lips. I was relieved in more than one way.

"Thanks for coming. You too Hitch. I'm sorry I messed up your plans for today. I didn't want to have my mom call out of work for nothing. My arm's not broken, just badly sprained."

I wanted to say screw my plans and throw myself at her knees as her humble servant, but I refrained.

"What happened?" Hitch asked.

"Yeah," I echoed, wishing I would've asked first, "what happened?"

She looked around to make sure no one was listening, scrutinizing the waiting room with slitted eyes. "I better tell you guys outside," she said, taking my hand and moving toward the exit.

Before we stepped out of the hospital, tears overflowed from the corners of her eyes. "It was a tree."

I wrapped my arm around her shoulders. "It's okay. You're safe now," I said, exchanging glances with Hitch.

She looked up at me with scared blue eyes. "For how long Knox?! I should hate you right now, but . . . I don't, I can't."

I hugged her closer to me as we walked to the car. I winked at Hitch, signaling for help with Evelyn.

"We'll figure this out," he promised. "Tell us what happened. Every little detail."

"I was going on my lunch break when the apple tree in front of Chubby's toppled over. The police said, if it weren't for the restaurants' overhang it would've crushed me. I heard the tree falling before I saw it. I tried to get out of the way but got knocked off balance by a branch and fell onto the sidewalk on my arm."

I gave Hitch the keys to drive and got in the back seat with Evelyn. Evelyn went over the details of her lunch break twice on the way to my house, making sure she didn't leave out anything that could be helpful.

My mother greeted us with less than her usual zest. She was clearly not happy to see Evelyn, but upon noticing her arm was in a sling, she lightened up.

"Oh my, what happened?!"

"She fell at work mom," I said before Evelyn could tell her anything to the contrary.

I took Evelyn's coat and purse and hung it on the coat rack and had her take a seat on the couch with Hitch while I spoke to my mother in the kitchen. The kitchen still smelled like cookies. A smell I normally loved, but now it tied a knot in the pit of my stomach, making me feel nauseous.

"Knox, I'm sorry the girl got hurt, but that's no reason to leave Mr. Brentley's so rudely. You should've said where you were going."

"You're right Mom, I'm sorry."

You would've thought I brought home a stray dog with the way my mother shook her head at me. "I feel awful she's hurt but did you have to bring her here?"

"Mom, I know you don't like her—"

"I never said that."

"Mom . . ."

She crossed her arms over her chest.

"Lincoln, Evelyn, and I all made up before Lincoln's death," I said, lying to my mother for her own good. "There's no reason to dislike Evelyn for what she did when she was a kid. And she means a lot to me. I'd like you to try to like her. Try for me Mom?"

She glanced at Evelyn from the kitchen "Oh Knox."

"Please Mom," I wined, tugging on her shirt sleeve. That seemed to do the trick.

"For you, I will."

"Good, Hitch and I have to step out and I want you to keep Evelyn company."

She frowned and for the first time I realized my mother was old. "We'll be really quick. Half an hour tops." I leaned in and pressed a kiss to her cheek. "I love you, Mom. I don't say it enough."

She blushed, pushing me away. "Oh Knox, I love you too." Opening a Tupperware container of cookies, she placed a handful on a plate. "Sometimes I think I love you too much, if there's such a thing. I'd do anything for you. You know that."

I let her kiss my cheek without making a fuss and together we walked back into the living room.

"Evelyn, Hitch and I have to run out really quick. My mom's going to keep you company."

She looked at Hitch then back at me. "I can't go with you?"

"No, I think you should stay here."

Evelyn didn't put up a fight and I was glad of it.

My mom took the vacant seat on the couch next to Evelyn. "Have a cookie. The boys helped me make them this morning."

I inclined my head toward the front door. Hitch snatched a cookie, popping it into his mouth, before getting to his feet. We grabbed our coats and headed outside.

I exploded as soon as we were off the front porch and no longer in hearing distance. "Hitch, I'm freaking out right now!" Pointing at him in frustration, "You can't tell me you don't believe my tree is a freaking killing tree. I told you; *the truth is stranger than fiction!*"

"Do not quote Lord Byron at me right now," Hitch said, his voice cracking. "I'm with you all the way buddy. I'm freaking out too."

I leaned against a tree in the front yard and looked to the overcast sky for answers. "How are we going to save Evelyn?"

"I don't know."

I held myself together in front of Evelyn but now I had no control. I covered my face with my hands. "What did I do?! I killed my brother and now I'm going to kill Evelyn. Hitch, I need your help now more than ever!"

He put his hand on my shoulder. "I really don't know what to do."

I shut my eyes to collect my thoughts. The moment my lids closed, Lincoln's dead eyes stared at me.

I swallowed, opening my eyes to look at Hitch through splayed fingers and fogging glasses. "I saw Lincoln."

Hitch furrowed his eyebrows. "What are you talking about?"

"I thought he was a figment of my concussion but what if he wasn't? Maybe you're right and the white orbs are spirit orbs. What if he's one of them? —A ghost. We can ask him for help."

"Um okay," Hitch said, "and how do we do that?"

"I saw him by the tree, when I fainted."

Hitch slung his backpack over his shoulder, "Let's go. We'll do what we planned to. We'll cut the fence and walk Mr. Brentley's property and look for your brother."

We stopped at the Dodge to get the bolt cutters.

"How about you boys help with the trees instead of running around with that damn camera all day," my father barked at us, coming from the garage.

I shoved the bolt cutters into Hitch's backpack. "We will Dad. I promise."

"I've been hearing a lot of promises coming from you Knox. When are you going to make good on them?"

"Soon Dad, I promise."

He shook his head at us and went into the tree farm with a pair of pruning shears. Hitch and I ran in the opposite direction to The Killing Tree.

* * *

We stood in front of my tree, its shadow hovering over us like a harbinger of death.

"I feel silly saying it after everything that's happened," Hitch told me in a low voice, "but when I first saw this tree, I got this strange feeling, like I wanted to wish for something. And that was before you told me you wished Lincoln dead."

I raked over him in amazement. "Really, you did? What did you want to wish for?"

"Yeah, I did. But after you told your story to the camera, I didn't. I don't know, I guess this whole time I *did* believe it and was lying to myself and you to make us both feel better because: *one can't believe impossible things.*"

I gave a faint smile. That was from *Through the Looking Glass* by Lewis Carroll. "*Why, sometimes I've believed as many as six impossible things before breakfast.*"

Hitch returned the attempt at a smile, his eyes going to the tree. His expression was one of respect and reverence. He didn't tell me what he was going to wish for, and I didn't ask again.

He pulled out his camera and turned it on.

"Let's not incriminate ourselves," I said. "Don't start filming until I'm done cutting the fence.

"Good thinking," Hitch said, the camera light now blinking red.

I took the bolt cutters and snipped the fence just enough so I could slip through. Once on the other side, I pulled the fence back for Hitch and the camera.

"The spirit orbs may not go through the branches without you making a wish. Repeat your wishes for the camera."

I put my hand on my tree from Mr. Brentley's side of the fence and repeated my first wish. I wasn't wearing gloves. The rough bark felt so familiar as if I never went to California. "I wish my brother was dead."

Hitch timed out ten minutes on his watch, and I repeated my third wish. "I wish for Evelyn Butler to live a long and healthy life."

"Okay," Hitch said, "that's a wrap."

Before heading home, we walked around Mr. Brentley's tree farm looking for anything out of the ordinary and finding nothing. Besides his trees being in desperate need of pruning, it appeared to be a perfectly normal tree farm. There was no sign of Lincoln. I didn't know how I was going to ask him for help, if I couldn't see him.

When we got back to the house my mom was still sitting with Evelyn. She got up to greet me with a kiss. "Glad you boys are back. I'm going to start dinner."

"Okay Mom."

"Whacha making, Mrs. L?" Hitch asked.

"Meatloaf, I hope that's okay?"

He hung up his coat and rubbed his belly. "I love meatloaf.

You're a lucky boy Knox. My mom's idea of cooking is ordering a pizza."

My mom smiled graciously before rushing off to the kitchen.

"You're laying it on a little thick, don't you think?"

"I already warned you about my intentions toward your mother," he teased.

"You find anything?" Evelyn asked, giving me a hug as soon as my mother was out of sight.

"I don't know."

I looked to Hitch.

"On it."

Evelyn and I huddled in front of the TV as Hitch plugged in his camcorder. We watched the footage discouraged. When I repeated the wish for Lincoln to die, the spirit orbs, like before, traveled up the tree and disappeared. The result was the same from both sides of the fence. We concluded they must go into the tree as they pass through the web-like branches, to which Hitch suggested we cut it down.

That didn't seem like a bad idea. Especially, because, after I made my wish for Evelyn to live a long and healthy life, nothing happened.

Evelyn was in near tears. She gripped my hand. After the tree at Chubby's, she, like the rest of us, knew that my second wish for her hadn't worked and for whatever reason the spirit orbs traveling into the tree were confirmation a wish would come true. We all knew Evelyn was going to die—soon.

I squeezed her hand. "I'm not going to let anything happen to you." I was lightheaded at the thought. For a second, I thought I was going to faint.

Instantly, I perked up, anxiety coursing through my veins like a 24-Hour energy drink. "I have an idea!"

"Mom," I called from the threshold of the kitchen, "we're

going to my room."

"Okay," she called back from the stove, "I'll call you when dinner's done."

The three of us went upstairs to my bedroom. I closed the door behind us in a hurry. "Hitch, I want you to knock me out."

"Say what?!"

"I saw Lincoln when I fainted. I need you to help me get back to that state—somewhere between sleep and waking, so I can talk to him."

"You saw Lincoln's ghost?!" Evelyn asked.

I nodded, focusing on Hitch.

His eyebrows were right angles on his face. "How do you suppose I do that?"

"Yeah Knox, he can't punch you in the face, your mother would kill him."

"Nothing like that Evelyn."

I spoke to Hitch in a language he would understand. "Remember in *The Princess Bride* when the Dread Pirate Roberts puts Andre the Giant in the sleeper hold by wrapping his arms around his neck? You're going to do that to me until I pass out. As soon as I lose consciousness, release your grip or you'll actually kill me."

I looked to Evelyn. "Let him know when I'm out."

Evelyn spoke wearily, "I don't like this."

"We have to Evelyn. Lincoln is our last hope."

I shouldn't have said that out loud, I knew that, but it had slipped out and it was the truth.

"Okay," she said, "I'll let him know when you've passed out."

Being taller than Hitch, I got down on my knees so he could have easy access to my neck from behind me. I felt his inner elbow lock around my neck. I smiled reassuringly at Evelyn. She gently took off my glasses and brushed back my hair before touching her lips to mine. She looked so beautiful there in my room. I thought it had to be a dream. The edges of my vision blurred, I blinked. I blinked again.

Lincoln was standing in front of me. If it weren't for his pale pallor and the tell-tale cut across his cheek he'd received the day the tree crushed him, I would've thought he was alive.

"Lincoln, thank God. I need your help!"

"If I could help you, I would. The best thing I can do is watch over Evelyn when she gets here."

"I can't let her die. I love her."

"I know," he said, his face twisting into a frown "I know." He tried to touch my shoulder, but his hand went through it. I felt nothing.

"Be careful Knox, Mr. Brentley knows you've been in his yard."

"How?"

"Your friend is right; the white orbs are spirits, and they go through the dead tree at the end of our property. It's a shortcut to his house and they tell him everything. Knox, you have to promise me you won't go. Please don't go. I don't want him to hurt you. I've never gone, I'm too scared. I stay at the house with Mom and Dad mostly. And now that you're here, I've been following you."

"You can't leave—can't move on?"

"I don't know how. None of us do."

"I forgive you Lincoln."

"I know and I forgive you."

My heart felt like it was going to wear out. "I'm so sorry. I love you so much. I never meant for this to happen. I miss my best friend."

"I know Knox, I love you too. I'm happy you finally came to visit."

"I'll visit from now on. I promise. I promise. I promise . . ."

I came through in a daze, tears streaming down my cheeks. I scanned the room for Lincoln. He was gone.

My wits about me, I jumped to my feet and darted to the bedroom door. Lincoln didn't think he could help, but he did. I now knew what he meant when he said don't go. It wasn't don't go back to California it was don't go to Mr. Brentley's. He confirmed Mr. Brentley was at the heart of The Killing Tree. There was a link between The Killing Tree, Mr. Brentley, and the spirit orbs. If anyone could help Evelyn, it was Mr. Brentley.

"Where are you going?!" Hitch and Evelyn asked at the same time.

I took my glasses from Evelyn and planted a kiss on her cheek, "I'll be right back."

I ran down the steps, "Mom, be back in a few. I have to go to the store."

I grabbed my coat and the keys to the Dodge and went out the front door. I drove up the street and parked on the side of the road. I didn't want to risk my dad seeing the Dodge parked at Mr. Brentley's.

I bounded up the porch and rang Mr. Brentley's doorbell.

Before my finger left the button, he opened the door with a smile. It was as if he had been waiting for me.

"My mom thought I should apologize after how rudely I left this morning. May I come in?"

He opened the door without hesitation. "I was wondering when you were going to come alone."

I entered. We stood in the foyer. A large chandelier with glass crystals hanging from its many brass arms caught the little bit of light that still filtered in through the windows.

"You know everything in this town, so I assume you know why I'm really here?"

"You want to save Evelyn Butler."

"Tell me how. I know you know how. It's your tree that's making this happen."

"Come," he said, leading me into the sheet covered living room. He held his cane under his arm and whipped the sheet covering the couch off like a matador tempting a bull. "The tree you call The Killing Tree is not mine." He neatly folded the sheet and placed it on the couch before taking a seat next to it. He let his cane rest between his legs. I noticed the couch was made of solid wood. The tufted cushions down to the buttons on them were all wood. This puzzled me. I had never seen anything like it. The craftsmanship was superb, but the execution made no sense. Who would want a wooden couch no matter how beautifully carved it was? Upon further examination, I noticed the legs of the couch came up from the hardwood floor like vines. My mouth became dry. A cold sweat beaded like morning dew in my hairline. They weren't vines at all—they were tree roots.

I removed the sheet covering the chair next to where Mr. Brentley sat. It too was the product of tree roots shooting out of the floor and twisting into furniture. In a frenzy, I went around the room pulling off all the sheets. I pulled up the sheet I had peaked under earlier that day. The globe and its base were also part of the tree. I yanked off the sheet from the wooden frame above the fireplace mantel. Encircled by roots that had twisted into an ornate pattern resembling a fishtail braid, was a portrait of a middle-aged Mr. Brentley before his dark hair had turned gray. His green eyes cut through me. There was something so familiar about the painting. I just couldn't put my finger on it.

"What is this?! What is all of this?!"

Mr. Brentley spoke calmly as if he didn't just watch me rip apart his living room. "The Killing Tree has the power to do great things."

"Evil things!" I shouted, pacing the living room. My body felt like a live wire. Every inch of me pulsated with nervous energy. My jaw twitched. "Tell me how to stop it. It killed my brother and now it's going to kill Evelyn."

"No," Mr. Brentley said in the same calm voice. "You killed your brother."

He confirmed my worse fear. My hands tightened into wrecking balls at my sides. "I didn't mean it."

"You did, even if it was only for a fraction of a moment, you did, and the tree granted your inner most desire, but you already know that Knox."

Mr. Brentley leaned forward, resting his chin on the top of his cane. "I tried to warn you when you were a little boy. I knew one day you would be drawn to the tree just as I was."

My head was spinning. "I don't understand," I said, not sure if it was tears or sweat dripping down my face. "I wished for Evelyn Butler to live a long and healthy life, and I mean that more than anything, but she almost died today."

"Yes Knox, you wished for her to live a long and healthy life, but that wasn't your first wish, and that is where the problem lies. The tree will grant you only one wish for each person. Your wish for Evelyn Butler to die is the one and only wish the tree will answer regarding young Evelyn Butler."

"I sat down next to Mr. Brentley, covering my face with my hands. It was tears now. "She'll die and there's nothing I can do about it?"

"I'm afraid so, son."

I looked to him desperately. "What if I chopped it down and burned it?"

"It wouldn't change a thing. The tree has roots all over Elwood. There's no stopping it."

I wiped my tears with the back of my coat sleeve. "Those

white orbs, are they all people who've died because of the tree?"

"Yes," he said in a whisper.

"And they're all trapped here?"

"Elwood is their home. They wouldn't wish to be anywhere else."

I stood up, facing Mr. Brentley where he sat. I thought about what Hitch said about his impulse to make a wish the first time he saw the tree. "My mother didn't buy Lansbury Tree Farm from you, did she? You gave her the land to own and operate as a tree farm knowing people would walk past the killing tree and make a wish."

I took Mr. Brentley's cane and pointed it at him. "That's what you want! You want people to die?!"

"That's not what the tree was intended for. But it seems to be human nature to want to destroy. When given their most inner desire, mankind aims at hurting themselves. I suppose it's kill or be killed."

He pushed the cane away from his face. "There's no shame in giving into the most basic human perversion Knox. I, myself, have many times."

I pawed at my face, still holding his cane. "How old are you really?"

"As old as the tree and yet older."

He stood up, seizing my arm. "Be careful of what you wish for Knox. I tried to warn you once, please heed it now."

I tore myself free and pushed his cane into his hands. "Some people never learn."

CHAPTER NINE
A Wish

I left Mr. Brentley's in a stupor. I forgot that I had parked down the street and staggered home, crossing through my family's tree farm.

Evelyn was going to die and just like Lincoln it was because of me. I couldn't let that happen. I was going to save Evelyn and make sure something like this never happens again. I was going to burn the tree down. Even if it only bought us time. It was better than nothing. And when it grew back, I would burn it down again.

I grabbed a gas tank from the garage and went to The Killing Tree. I was operating on nerves. It seemed like I flew from the garage to my tree and was again standing under its shadow. "Never again," I said to it with the same firm voice of Mr. Brentley as I poured gasoline over its's trunk. I didn't care if the entire farm caught fire. I was being reckless.

I threw a lit match and waited. Within seconds the trunk was engulfed in a golden flame. The heat felt good, and it felt good doing something.

Just as quickly as the tree caught fire, it went out. Not even a scorch mark was detectable on its gray bark.

The smell of gasoline and smoke from my failed execution filled my nostrils. I felt dizzy and nauseous at the same time. The ground spun under me. I put my hand on my knees to steady myself. I was going to faint for real this time.

I heard Lincoln. "It's not going to work." His voice, like his image, went in and out of focus as I fought passing out.

In the twilight, the light bent around the trees giving the impression my brother was solid. It was the perfect example of refraction. It gave me another idea. It looked like science *could* solve my problem after all.

I smiled at Lincoln. "No, it's not going to work, but you reminded me of a lesson Mr. Brentley taught me when I was little—things aren't always what they seem."

His eyes were alive with hope. "What are you going to do?"

"I'm going to make a wish."

I touched The Killing Tree like an old friend, for that was what it was. It had seen me through my adolescence and had granted me my foolish heart's desire. It had done it for me. I hoped it would do this last thing for its old friend. Just as the light bent around Lincoln, I would bend my next wish to my will. "I wish for Mr. Brentley to bear the full burden of Evelyn Butler's fate."

The wind whipped through the tree farm rustling the pine needles. The sound was something almost sweet, yet sad. I took a deep breath and turned to Lincoln. He was gone.

Still feeling woozy, I headed back to my parents' house. I had just made it onto the front porch when I heard a thunderous cracking. I turned my head toward Mr. Brentley's. I knew what it was.

My father was the first one through the front door. Seeing me, he wrapped me in a bear hug. "When I heard that noise . . . I thought . . ." he said, not able to finish his sentence as a sob broke free.

"It's okay Dad, I'm fine. I think the sound came from Mr. Brentley's."

I was taken aback by my father, by his tears. I thought he hated me after what happened to Lincoln, I guess I was wrong, and I was never happier to be.

My father released me, pawing at his tears. My mother, Hitch, and Evelyn were on the porch now. My mother grabbed my hand, "Knox what was that?"

My father answered for me. "Knox thinks the sound came from Mr. Brentley's. Come on boys, let's go check it out."

We approached Mr. Brentley's on foot. Twilight had passed, giving rise to a grinning moon whose pale-yellow glow shone down upon my shoulders like a boulder. My father halted, thrusting out his hands to stop Hitch and me. We looked on toward Mr. Brentley's house. A huge Douglas Fir tree had fallen, crashing through his front window and crushing him to death.

CHAPTER TEN
The Day after Christmas

We were enjoying Christmas dinner leftovers for lunch when we heard a knock on the front door. "I'll get it," I said, pressing a kiss to the side of Evelyn's face before getting up.

"I didn't know the United States Postal Service worked the day after Christmas," I said to the woman at the door.

"Have to, there's just too much mail. I wish people would send Christmas cards, gifts, and everything else through the phone."

I signed for the certified letter anxiously, surprised it was for me. "Have a nice New Year," I said, shutting the door.

"Who was it honey?" My mother yelled from the kitchen.

"The mailman—uh, mailwoman—uh, mailperson."

"Anything from the Hitchcocks?" Hitch called to me from his seat. He was still waiting on a Christmas card from his parents.

"No," I said, examining the letter from the law offices of Davison and Sons. "Just junk mail."

I opened it to read:

Dear Mr. Knox Lansbury,

We offer you our sincerest condolences in lieu of the passing of Mr. K. Brentley. We, at the office of Davison and Sons,

will do all in our power to execute his wishes as he willed. We will be in contact with you over the estate in the next coming weeks. Please find included in this envelope a letter from Mr. K. Brentley to be delivered to you upon his death.
Sincerely,
 W. Davison.

I examined the small envelope enclosed with the letter from the lawyer. I was confused by it, more so than the letter from the lawyer. It had my name handwritten on it.
I glanced into the kitchen, making sure my absence wasn't felt and then carefully opened the letter, making sure not to tear it. Inside the letter was a house key and a single piece of stationery. It read:

My dearest boy,
I warned you to be careful of what you wished for, a warning you did not heed.
Go back to California and become a doctor and when you graduate return to Elwood. It's not only your legacy but your destiny.
When medicine fails or just simply because you can, send the lost souls to the tree. Remember Knox, *Death is the crown of life. Were death denied, poor men would live in vain. Were death denied, to live would not be life. Were death denied, every fool would wish to die.*

Your brother and I will be waiting,
Your loving father,
Knox Brentley

CHAPTER ELEVEN
The Truth

Around of applause sounded, the claps growing until they were deafening. Hitch stood, taking a bow and giving me a wink. I faked a smile for his benefit and did my best to clap enthusiastically, standing with the rest of the crowd to give him a standing ovation.

Hitch's senior project, *The Killing Tree,* was a success. He could sleep peacefully tonight, but I couldn't. I was restless. My hand felt the key to Mr. Brentley's house in my pocket, the cool metal doing its part to smooth the desire that was burning in my core.

Mr. Brentley was waiting for me and so was Lincoln. I felt the pull of the tree more than ever and more than ever I felt the need to make a wish. Mr. Brentley had told me the tree wasn't his, that's right, it wasn't—it was mine.

I never told Hitch or Evelyn the wish I made for Mr. Brentley and never told them Mr. Brentley was my father. They thought a tree killing mean, old Mr. Brentley was a coincidence and the run-ins with trees Evelyn had experienced were the same. When Evelyn made it through the rest of winter break without incident, they laughed at their silliness. And how silly they must have been to think a tree could grant wishes.

I laughed along. I'd been doing a lot of that lately. Doing my best to be a chameleon and blend in as I bide my time. I glanced at Mrs. Butler as she stood next to Evelyn, clapping. Hitch had flown them in for the movie premiere and I was glad he did. I smiled at Mrs. Butler, she returned the expression, sending my heart into palpitations. She would be next. Months later it still bothered me how she gossiped about my mother with Hitch. If she was gossiping to Hitch, who she'd just met, who else was she gossiping to? She insinuated my mother slept with Mr. Brentley to get the tree farm.

Maybe it bothered me because there was truth to it. There was no denying Mr. Brentley was my father. Lincoln was named after the man *I thought* was my father, and I was named after Mr. Brentley. The painting that hung over Mr. Brentley's fireplace mantle was familiar to me, because it looked like me. I had his piercing green eyes.

Mr. Brentley owned Elwood; he could have given my mother any piece of property he chose. He gave her the property next to his to watch his son. I was wrong when I accused Mr. Brentley of giving my parents the tree farm as a way to lure people to The Killing Tree. That honor was mine.

I was going home for the summer before medical school started in the fall, and I knew the first thing I was going to do once home was march up to my tree and wish for Mrs. Butler to die. I didn't like her gossiping, and I didn't like Mrs. Butler. She was a burden to my Evelyn and Evey would be better off without her.

I was no longer haunted by Lincoln's face when I closed my eyes. Once I accepted who and what I was, the sting of remorse and the weight of guilt lifted.

I'm a killer. The truth is I am a serial killer. I killed my own father and my only brother, and I knew I would kill Mrs. Butler and after her, I'd kill again. I thought I'd decided to become a doctor to save lives, but the truth was darker. I was becoming a doctor so I would have the power to save and the power to take and in that, know the value in taking. It's just like my father said, The Killing Tree was not only my legacy but my destiny. I would make a wish and another one because I could, and in doing so honor the final lesson my father taught me: Death is the crown of life.

The End . . .

THANKS FOR READING!

If this book helped you escape, if only for a moment, please consider taking the time to leave a review or star rating on Amazon or whatever platform you use. It would warm the cockles of my little, black heart to hear from you.

Looking for something else to read? Don't forget to check out my other books on Amazon.

Follow me on social media (I'm on all platforms under Holly Knightley). Sign up for my newsletter for the latest news, glimpse into my wacky process, and occasional freebie. Stay spooky and happy reading!

WANT MORE?